CW01065574

Go Gentle

Also by David Peak

No 4 Pickle Street

The Cotoneaster Factor

Go Gentle

David Peak

To John,
   In fond memory of quants and mr. Pett.

   With best wishes,
         Dave Peak
      21st March 1991

FOURTH ESTATE · London

First published in Great Britain by
Fourth Estate Limited
289 Westbourne Grove
London W11 2QA

Copyright © 1991 by David Peak

The right of David Peak to be identified as author of this
work has been asserted by him in accordance with the Copyright,
Designs and Patents Act 1988.

A catalogue record for this book
is available from the British Library

ISBN 1-872180-23-X

All rights reserved. No part of this publication may be reproduced,
transmitted or stored in a retrieval system, in any form or by any
means, without permission in writing from Fourth Estate Limited.

Typeset in Bembo by York House Typographic, Hanwell, W7.
Printed and bound by Billings Ltd, Worcester

Monday Evening

And she was calling from the doorway something like, *Don't forget the milk or we'll have none for breakfast.* He remembers squeezing through a black gate, shaking his head at the absurdity of her command. It was some other home, not his. He followed the wet pavement beside a carriageway jammed with traffic. Dimly coloured clouds were flowing too quickly overhead; and from several lighted windows on the left, elderly people were scrutinising the beginning of his journey, smiling to themselves. Then the unclear part: as he turned the corner towards the shop he found himself in a darkness so complete he could touch it, feel it brushing his face. He was woken then by the pain of something striking his shoulder. A bird maybe. Flapping for a moment, then falling at his feet.

'And that's all I can remember. The hangover of it's been with me all day.'

Miriam hadn't been listening. 'How you manage to make such a mess in a room this size, I'll never know.'

He turned to watch as she tidied magazines and

rearranged his fruit to prevent the grapes being bruised.

'It comes naturally.'

As soon as she was satisfied there was nothing more to be done in the way of tidying she glanced at her watch and stood over him, her hands linked in front of her.

'I'd better be off now. They'll be ringing the bell any moment.' Stooping towards him without bending her knees, she kissed his cheek. 'I'll be in again tomorrow. You get some rest now.'

For the second time he caught a perfume of creams and her lover's moisture.

'Tomorrow? What about the zoo?'

'Didn't I tell you? I've taken some leave. I'm off till next Monday now.'

'What time will you come then?'

'Oh, you know. Whenever.'

He nodded. 'I'll make sure I'm in.'

She moved to the door with the precision of a ballerina, turning at the last moment to smile. He raised his hand. And could it have been . . . a sparkle in her eye as the door swung shut?

Miriam, you amuse me, like Jeff the other day with his paperback and bag of Spanish oranges.

Jim's room was now no bigger than the kitchen back home. Dull tints of town night were hanging against its windows. As usual the beast had woken at his wife's kiss and was making its own hillock in the hospital blanket. It should be dissuaded from any display of grandeur before Miranda came to sedate him. For a moment he was foreseeing her dark hair coiled in its cardboard cap, that sweetheart backside tightening the lilac uniform and her eyes at this time of night like those of Lucifer as a man comes crawling through shafts of darkness from one living to another. Perhaps she has someone dear to her called Norman who drops round to her place the moment she's back from work, bringing with him a box of chocolates and roses made of icing sugar. Does he then woo her with a promenade to the chip shop and back? Salt and vinegar? A pickled egg? And does she walk reluctantly at his side noticing how streetlights illuminate the cod grease on his fingers as he eats from unfolded newspaper and tells her of his day? Yes, the exhaust will have fallen off his Fiesta and the screwball at the garage will have overcharged him. If Miranda does have a boyfriend christened Norman then those in service professions will always be taking advantage of him and he'll have frequent need to seek her advice on his lack of self-assertion.

Towards midnight my skies fill with sequins of imagination.

Tuesday

i

Usually the moment of waking was all words but today, with blocked nose and a morning glory, Jim surfaced warm and flat on his back, a milk sky against the window and the hum of machinery – unheard other than at this hour – from the hospital basement. His room was dull, and slightly smaller than before. He was biting his gums at the memory of Miriam's relatives, who'd come to see him in pairs over the course of his first few days only to hold table-tennis conversations with each other – Jim the net – toss, serve, a little backspin, rally. Buggers, buggers. An ailment of this kind was a fine subject when it struck like an arrow in the dark, but not when you could see it whistling up the avenue with your suitcase in its hand. Hold the bat sideways on to give the ball an unpredictable swerve. And in the course of a meeting with Miriam to consider the drawing-up of his will, her interest had soon strayed – not that it mattered – onto the lump sum she'd receive when this ailment finally rapped on his door. Certainly there'd been traces of childhood in her eyes when the subject came up. The amount was unimportant, of course, and the only thing he should worry about was pulling himself together and abandoning the idea of deterioration altogether, but she refused to see the funny side when he explained – as if it needed explaining – that human beings hadn't yet mastered that particular ruse.

The staff on lates last night were on earlies this morning, following what Miranda called the 'quick change-over'. She was in a frenetic mood – brought on by a lack of sleep, Norman, or both, who could tell? – and veered towards the hysterical, with much incongruous chuckling and a bunching-up of Devil eyes as her showered body reached over him to adjust his pillows, though there was no need. His face was pressed against her uniform, her perfume resuscitating some dark side of his soul, and the beast itself. The damn thing has no respect. He was outlining his hopes for the day while a slice of him out of sight had chosen her as a suitable recipient for dawn's first need and was preparing itself for a conquest which wouldn't come. On this occasion, as on every other, she noticed, brushed against, and generally tolerated his excitement, as nurses will, though this niggled him because in life he preferred to be looked upon as a decent chap – the kind one comes across on news reports who stays behind after a major accident, despite broken limbs, to rescue strangers and who later shrugs off the attention of the tabloids. Her armpits were already damp and for the time it took her to plump his pillows he was loath to rescue his nose from this one on the left, with its sweetness of soap above bitters of a more primitive kind.

Since admission he'd had in his cabinet an instrument similar in shape to a section of car exhaust but, despite this, he always took pains to use the bathroom across the corridor, on the basis that this brought him self-esteem. Making the journey he would notice more than at any other time a reluctance in his limbs to do as they were asked, and a lethargy about them, as if he were a battery inadvertently left outside in a cold snap. And it was often difficult to ascertain whether his foot would bother to reach the floor each time he stepped forwards. On arrival at the bathroom he'd sit on the toilet in a state of great calm. By some unknown process this energy loss took place in selected areas, leaving hands, head and the beast untouched – a fortunate trio from which he could still elicit scraps of pleasure – poor Miranda generally the centre of them, though he took care to forgive himself afterwards; and in some ways he subsequently enjoyed a sense of physical companionship with her.

Yes so, *this* proportion of the insurance money would be used to pay for a comfortable funeral. He'd already selected a casket from the catalogue brought in by the undertaker, who'd been gratified by this opportunity to small-talk with a future client. Yes, Jim could, if he so wished, take with him his signed copy of *The Country Girls*; and yes, the undertaker had had words with the vicar and it seemed more than likely Jim could be interred if not *directly* beneath the hawthorn then at least in proximity to it. Roots were often a problem, as he could appreciate. He would then know – if knowing were part and parcel of being No More – that he was lying close to one of the spots he'd once conversed with Laura on golden, secret afternoons.

In terms of the casket itself – not wishing to squander too much of Miriam's coming fortune – Jim had chosen what would have been called in supermarket circles, *This Week's Special Offer*. It would be a nonsense to waste cash on an object designed to spend the majority of its time out of sight, and at this opinion the undertaker nodded without enthusiasm. It was beginning to appear that everyone other than Jim was viewing his bleak destiny as a special occasion deserving of the best, while the client himself would have been happy with a large, adapted teachest conveyed to the churchyard on the roofrack of a rusting Vauxhall Chevette. Once Miriam had settled the details, Jim toyed with the idea of writing his own funeral oration; but he hadn't yet been able to strike the right note between solemnity and that popular black gratitude. The speech – each time he put pen to paper – invariably began: *Hi there, every bastard one of you*, underlined. Though he might have opted for this in the long run, the unlikely prospect of Laura turning up and sneaking into the rear pews prevented a firm decision. Then again, he couldn't shake off the notion that such a rigorous deliverance would at least provide the best opportunity for some time of being able to speak his mind without Miriam thereafter looking at him funny while thumbing through that month's copy of *Zoo Illustrated*. She had developed an admirable strength, though much of it must have come from Christopher, who had something Jim hadn't mastered – the ability to cheer Miriam up. Indeed it now appeared his efforts in this direction had been misguided; that all along passing-on was the one ploy he hadn't considered.

ii

Miranda was recording observations onto a chart she'd unhooked from the bottom of the bed. Her wrist appeared thin, translucent, as it manipulated the pen. He could see threads of vein beneath her almond skin and still detect those shower smells, rub-a-dub-dub up and up the night-grey thighs. She had become less frenetic, succumbed to a more conventional tiredness. Her eyes watered. Sitting up in his bed, Jim had a view of metal chimneys, flat roofs and, beyond these, the tips of the town: a milk lagoon of gables, spires, the dome of the old picture palace, aerials roosted by starlings and seagulls. Replacing his chart, Miranda moved to the window and wound the handle which operated an upper vent, letting in sounds of traffic, a rattle of distant road-diggers, a breath of cool town air, then stood with her arms on the sill looking out. Twice during her shift she would listen to him through a stethoscope, keeping one eye on the sphygmomanometer whose mercury thumped in tune with his heart till she turned a screw on the rubber bulb and released the pressure. As she replaced the equipment in its box her bottom would push out like a harvest apple and for those few seconds a sweet sweat would rise to the surface of his palms. She'd poke a thermometer under his tongue, check his pulse beneath two fingers, count his respiration rate. He looked forward to all this. Now she was watching the town, unaware, perhaps, of how tightened-up it had become overnight, dragging still closer the horizon of wooded hills.

'You look as if you'd rather be in bed, Miranda.'

He thought she replied 'Who knows?' but didn't bother asking her to clarify it. He was examining the shape of her back, the subtleties of her waist which somehow echoed the folds of the hills beyond.

'Still, I'm glad you're here.'

'Make the most of me. I have a day off tomorrow.

Can you believe it? A whole day. The bed and I will be thoroughly re-acquainted I can tell you.'

He couldn't think how to respond – a problem he often had in conversation. The darkness of her tights at the back of her legs and the paleness of skin beneath were drowning one another.

'I wouldn't mind a cup of tea.'

'Doris'll be along in a minute. She was just starting at the other end when I came in.'

Sighing, she turned away from the window, asked him if there was anything else he needed and, at the shake of his head, left the room. With the click of the door he realised how he could have enlivened the conversation and was quickly regaining a fluency he often had alone. Perhaps he could have employed it to shatter the barrier between patient and nurse. Thinking has cycles which roar, whimper. There was a lot to consider, resurrect, put in some kind of order.

Yes, words in the mornings, strings of them, often out of context – though a slight but persistent chill the last few days had granted them added significance. *Laura* – probably the most common of them, a mixture of vowels, soft consonants. Again and again for no reason he'd say *Laura* under his breath.

He'd had compliments about his shoulders long ago, the way their blades moved easily beneath his skin. And about the sculpture of his neck and fingers, fingers intended for delicate pastimes not undertaken. And his arms: how they'd once hung brown and tender from summer T-shirts. It had been suggested a few years back that he should pose for life classes but he'd been dissuaded by unmentioned spots on the smooth parts of his upper thighs and by concern that he might be over-influenced by those splashed art girls holding out their pencils at him. Now most of it was coming to an end. Through the briefest lives questions outweigh understanding or simple response. The globe has a way with her, always one reasoning ahead, amused by these antics, a mother still green and eternally patient.

The door was banged open by Doris's backside, itself followed by a tea-trolley holding an urn, a few dozen carefully balanced cups, a column of saucers, jug of milk, bowl of sugar cubes and a tin of cheap biscuits – about five quid a ton, dry as alum, with bumps on one side specially for the sick. She was plump and blue with white hair partially covered by the domestic equivalent of a plastic shower-cap. Having expressed pleasantries she poured his tea, rattled the cup onto his cabinet, poked a couple of biscuits onto the saucer, then wandered backwards through the door. Jim scratched his sternum and yawned, then sipped his tea and ate both biscuits as an experiment. There was no enjoyment to be had from eating these days. It was always a conscious thing, as if he were personally responsible for the success or otherwise of his own digestion but had forgotten the exact sequence of procedures. And then there was Laura, waiting as promised on the shadowy side of the church porch, her smile and amber hair the first things he noticed as he reached the top of the steps and came towards her, a clumsiness to his gait, which worsened as he tried to correct it, and a pain in his chest. And Miriam's voice: he could hear it as a second conscience tagging his progress along the path among snags of hawthorn, blue shadow, a symphony of birdsong from surrounding yews. He glanced up at the church tower, its castellations and coloured windows, then down at Laura, her legs drawn up onto the stone seat just inside the porch. As he came closer his attention was caught by a cobweb skirt, the crimson of her T-shirt, then dabs of light in her eyes like life itself. She was surprised he'd shown up. Awkwardly he hugged her, then sat opposite on the sunlit side, his legs open and his hands linked between them. Whatever he said and in whichever way he said it, she responded by laughing. She would neither confirm nor deny statements of sentiment, though she agreed it was difficult being opposite one another in such a sacred place. So they came out of the porch to follow the circular path through years of tombstones. In this fashion both of them were more at ease. He enjoyed glancing sideways to catch the side of her head, loved the musk of her as her hair brushed his shoulder, was uprooted by the shiver through his guts if her hand happened to touch his. The elderflowers were smelling of sweet champagne. His breath was over-conscious with the sparkle of her. Round the churchyard, then round again, posing as historians if someone came by, pointing at the gargoyles or the barred stained-glass windows . . . and he was conjuring excuses to tap her shoulder or press his mouth to the top of her head and pull strands of hair through his lips. Inconsequential things. She pretended. He was powerful and inordinately replete with humourisms. In silences she would laugh anyway and bump into his shoulder. Clouds of midges moved up and down, apparently aimless though she was sure there was a point to it. She'd read something about them. On the second or third circuit they came across the vicar, who lived in an ivy-covered house just visible through a narrow yellow gate. He diverted their attention for a moment with a commentary on God's roses, God's willow tree, God's general abundance. As he spoke a bee hummed through the flowerbed at his feet, then rose to encircle the grave of a child from the last century. Laura's skirt and T-shirt rippled in the breeze. The vicar said 'God be with you' as he fluttered towards the church. On the green, moist side of the graveyard they came across an old gentleman in black sitting on a bench cutting up newspaper with a large pair of scissors. He was placing each completed shape between the pages of a scrapbook to prevent them blowing away before he could glue them into position. Laura was looking at a window in the tower high above where a rusting metal cross had been clamped to the brickwork. As a child she'd been told the clamp was really a pair of braces belonging to a man who'd fallen from the window to his death. This uninscribed stone below marked the spot, and this old vase had once been filled with flowers by an unknown woman who came monthly to pay her respects. We guard children at our breast, yet they always grow. Laura laughed at the expression remaining on Jim's face as she finished her tale, digging her fingers into his waist. They turned round at the cry of the old gentleman, who was puffing along the path towards them. He pressed the shape of a newspaper moon into her hand and kissed her forehead. Later she sellotaped it to the dashboard of her car along with some old postcards from absent friends.

iii

Not that there'd been any children from the marriage. Something was wrong with Jim's sperms. It was Miriam's belief they were just selfish like the rest of him, but she'd stuck with him anyway, as if her purpose in living had been to choose those actions which would later give her good reason to grieve. Now and then they were in love soft as hammocks, but inevitably grieving took place and Jim, infected, became a griever too, though his spirit told him he wasn't one by nature. On grieving days he would squeal up the road on his way to work, beating the steering wheel with the nub of his palm and condemning Miriam to accidents of spontaneous combustion, killer buzzards, botulism in tins of tuna . . . and through all this, death, though not yet strolling along the avenue in full view, was round a corner making anonymous calls to parts of his body: an ache here; nausea there; spells of great lassitude burrowing almost to the marrow. Each symptom he saw as a psychosomatic response to the peaks and troughs of conflict and spiritual luxury he and Miriam experienced. Days of passion and gut-ache. For some time he'd been sleeping on a camp bed in Miriam's room, joining her only when softness came like a blindfold dove. In the mornings as they made themselves ready for work, they would meet in the middle of the kitchen for a peck, then carefully grill separate pieces of bread to the rhythm of Uncle Tobias thumping his slipper against the floor upstairs. Each day the three-mile drive to work helped restore Jim's equilibrium, enabling him to smile as he jangled through the door, waved good morning to Mei Lee (the refugee turned receptionist), hauled himself up the flight of stairs and came breathless into the open-plan, tropical-plant-filled Housing Benefit office. *What a bollock career.* And each day he glanced at the clock as he settled at his veneered desk, knowing that Miriam would have arrived at the zoo by then and would probably be feeding orang-utans, mucking out lions, or donning her works bikini to clean the inside of the glass terrapin pool. And two hours later he knew she'd be having coffee and Penguins with Christopher in the zoo café, sharing discontentments.

Living with Miriam was a simple, complex state of affairs, interwoven with dreams of the forbidden and the snores of Uncle Tobias sitting between them as the television flickered. Once a fortnight, say, a relative of Miriam's would ring to ask if there was any activity feasible for the coming weekend which would further cock up Jim's life, and if so they'd make arrangements for it that instant. To broaden his mind Jim bought jigsaw puzzles which he pieced together on a large square of hardboard kept under the wardrobe by day; snowy Canadian landscapes, or likenesses of masterpieces now known to have been painted by John Constable's brother Lionel. Jim liked to take this idea further to pass the time – maybe St Paul's had been the work of Sir Christopher's brother George – till Miriam thumped up the stairs in search of him and prowled in the doorway waiting for an opportunity to scratch at his motives, whereupon – though the discussion would begin quietly enough – he'd usually over-react to a single word and upset the snowy landscape or push her back and lock the door against her.

In his lunch-hours Jim sometimes consulted the problem pages of women's magazines to see if he could find similar marriages, and the general consensus seemed to be that this relationship was basically sound. It needed only a solution to certain problems, such as Christopher, the constant presence of disabled Uncle Tobias, and Jim's clandestine conversations with the jewel that was Laura. *Stay calm*, the magazines said. What would happiness be if it didn't contain its fair share of abject misery? *Unreal*, that's what it would be in Miriam's eyes – you only had to look at those couples wandering hand in hand round Primark. It was misguided of Jim to see them as privileged. They were simply having a break from the more rational happiness of conflict. No good would come from their apparent empathy, their shared senses of humour, the early morning croissants he imagined they consumed. Nevertheless, he was figuring – as the transient do – that given his time over again he might shy away from relationships which resembled having someone's fingers teasing the handle of a vice in which one's testicles rested, however much society claimed the anticipation of pain was a useful thing, given that it lured you into a suitably subservient state in which to welcome God later on. Through the ages men and women had preferred a God who enjoyed most of all to see His subjects pissed off. This was something Jim wanted to ask Him about if, following his demise, he found himself face to face with the Almighty. And doing his jigsaws, his mind free for the moment, he would wonder about death itself. Would it be bright with Bruce Kent lookalikes frolicking in streams of mineral water? Or would heaven be just an absence of the things he hadn't liked about being alive: market researchers, thistles, ex-public schoolboys eating duck in expensive restaurants, mucus, Albania, men whose chest and pubic hair formed one indivisible mat, those before-and-after photos in Sunday tabloids of people who had reduced excess fat by replacing their main meal with a cup of pink liquid tasting of irradiated strawberries, plain chocolate, or caramel.

Imagination faltering, Jim stood by the window watching pedestrians on the pavements below. The surrounding buildings were smaller now, though still in proportion to one another, and he could tell by the way they were moving that the townspeople, while not ignorant of the shrinkage which was taking place, were choosing not to make a fuss, stepping carefully over any ridges where the pavement had buckled and remaining happy to endure the slight inconvenience occasioned by the loss of an inch or so in its width overnight. Only the heavens seemed to have broadened, now clearing a little after a white dawn, the cloud cover parting here and there to reveal strands of blue and a light wind casually rearranging leaves which had fallen in the hospital garden. If he looked hard enough perhaps he'd see Laura, though she had long since gone away. Thinking of her he became like a statue against the window. They had parked in front of the Happy Burger restaurant. It was beginning to rain. She was showing him a book she'd bought. The date on the first page said 1803 and they were guessing whose hands the book had passed through in all the time since. Her knees were goosebumped with the weather, though she'd insisted on wearing her cobweb skirt and teasing his imagination with a different coloured T-shirt, yellow maybe. Yellow and a glimpse, if he leaned in a certain way, of her small breasts. Not that he leaned purposefully, but it happened sometimes during the shift of their conversation. Other cars were pulling off the road out of the worsening weather and shadows in raincoats were running at a stoop for the restaurant door. A mist had whitened the windows, showing mouths biting into burger buns, an agitation of children's cardigans, husbands tall and black unhooking wet coats from the shoulders of wives. What becomes the charm of one person creates agonies for another. Laura following raindrops with her finger in a more solemn mood than usual, prompting Jim to pick his words carefully as he touched the old book to enjoy the texture of its leather cover. Laura offered him a piece of chewing gum, then kissed his neck, making him curl like an injured spider.

The door opened. He could see in the surface of the window an image of Miranda.
'It's only me.'
She began to tidy his bed.
He tightened the cord of his dressing-gown, turned round and leant against the windowsill. She was re-making hospital corners with the bottom sheet.
'Bet you're getting sick to death of this room.'
A strand of dark hair had untwisted and was dancing against her ear.
'It wouldn't be so bad,' Jim said, 'if everything didn't have to be white.'
'White means clean. That's the idea.'
'And clean means everything's going well.'
'That's it in a nutshell.'
Though he'd recently wrapped a jumper round his Chinese alarm clock and hidden it in the cupboard, he could still hear its metallic tick as Miranda fussed over the bed, her bottom achieving the beauty of an apple cut in half. All his life he'd been dogged by appetite, but whenever he'd attempted to assuage it trouble brewed, making him realise the original hunger had been more of the spirit than the flesh though it usually came in flesh disguise. Apple shaped, and he

could rear against its skin, reach for its core with the tip of his tongue.

'There are biscuit crumbs all over the place. I don't know. You men!'

'Creating a mess is one of the few positive contributions we make in life. The rest is just a gradual revelation of our ineptitude.'

'Oh, you're *very* philosophical this morning, aren't you.'

'I think it has something to do with the build-up of medication.'

Standing upright, she extended her lower lip and exhaled. 'Well, that's another job over and done with. Perhaps if you could try not to twist around in it so much.'

She crinkled momentarily to stifle a yawn. Poking his hands into his dressing-gown pockets, Jim sat against the edge of the bed.

'I thought you were doing really well earlier on, Miranda, but now you look quite done in.'

'That was just my first wind. I've had it now. My fault. I went out for a meal after I'd finished last night.'

Jim lowered his chin. 'Norman?'

'What do you mean, "Norman"?'

'Just an invention of mine.' He patted her arm. 'A fictional boyfriend. Dependable chap with trousers the colour of . . . well, not quite grey and not quite brown. Functional trousers I'd call them. A nice fellow who'll take the day off work to put coving up in your bedroom, though he never manages to get the corners quite right. And he usually has a set of screwdrivers in the car, the ones with a single handle and a series of interchangeable shafts. He *loves* roast lamb. Buys those headache remedies advertised on

TV which turn out to have the same ingredients as every other headache remedy, just a different packet. He invariably has his width-fitting checked in A.G. Meek's, and he hasn't married because of something awful in his past which women discover when they're idling through his diary. Thinks oral sex means just talking about it. You know. *Norman.*'

'I think you're right about the medication.'

Jim coughed. 'Look. I don't want you to take this the wrong way. But I've been wanting to tell you – not for any reason, but just because of what are called *circumstances* – that you're a very attractive person.'

'Thanks, Jim, but I'm sure your condition is having an undue influence on your opinions.'

'No, I mean it.'

'Don't be offended, but the terminally ill are always paying me compliments. Gives me a complex. Be interesting to see if you changed your tune if you suddenly recovered.'

Jim examined his fingernails. 'I was only saying you were attractive. I wasn't asking you to marry me or anything.'

'Yes, but what does it mean? What are you trying to say? I've never understood the point of people telling me I'm attractive.'

'I don't think there is one as such. A point I mean.' He lay full-stretch on the bed as Miranda twisted in triumph and peered into the corridor.

'I almost forgot. Mr Cook is coming in to see you later.'

'Oh yes. And what does he want?'

'Don't worry. He rang just now saying he had some good news for you. You should feel honoured. It's not everyday a consultant deigns to come over this early in the day.'

Jim was yawning. 'He's probably realised he's mixed up my x-rays and I'm actually dying of something far less serious.'

'Don't get morose. It doesn't suit you.'

'Why shouldn't I? That's the trouble with living. Everyone's always telling you not to be morose. And just when you've packed it in the person who told you not to be morose gets morose themselves and comes round to your place to tell you about it for three hours over coffee, and worst of all, the things they're getting morose about are never half so bad as the ones *you* were getting morose about before they told you to cheer up.'

'Very amusing, I'm sure. No, Mr Cook wouldn't say what the good news was. He wanted to tell you himself. Anyway, you'll find out soon enough.'

Turning round, she glimpsed herself in the mirror and moved closer to study her face.

'Miranda. What I said just now. I didn't want it to be just flattery. You've been a great help to me and I suppose I was trying to express that. I think it's important people should know how special they are.'

She was attending to a spot. 'Well thank you, Jim. It's very kind of you.' She squeezed and laughed simultaneously. 'Let's just be thankful your wife isn't here to listen.'

'If you don't mind me saying so, that's a pretty typical response. And quite sad in its way.'

'I was only joking. You're trying to be funny and I was just going along with it.'

'It's annoyed me.'

'OK, I'm sorry.'

Now she was pinching the skin below her left eye, testing its elasticity. Her voice was casual and unconnected with him. 'This is the first time I've seen you irritable since you came in.'

'I admit it wasn't an original thing to say, but I *meant* it. It wasn't intended as a way round you or a device or anything like that.'

Leaving her skin alone, she quickly checked her profile then looked directly at him.

'OK, I believe you,' she said.

The door swung open. It was Sister, mauve and over-excited like a ripening plum.

'If you're not too busy, Nurse King, you're needed. Come with me.'

Puffing her cheeks, Miranda followed Sister out of the room. The plum was well known for hating her patients to such a degree that many recovered to spite her. And there were rumours she was having an affair with a Sister from the Fracture Clinic. Two fruits together. Jim sunk into his pillow, listening to footsteps hurrying up and down the corridor. Emergencies were invariably old men choking on vomit. No poets here, and the concealed alarm clock was affirming that time was a linear thing, when once it had swung and quickstepped in upon itself.

iv

A memory in particular of Miriam watching as he threw pebbles from a parapet into the river. The day coming green and moist through a line of elders. She was wearing jeans and a mulberry shirt, tight white shoes – more telling than showing when showing has the greater subtlety. Further up, beside the reservoir, young boys were angling and one of them landed a silver fish which sparkled in his wet hands. Later still Miriam was coming, fingers uprooting a tussock of goose-grass. Even then he could predict the family occasion which eventually turned up, fat with roast chicken, cigar smoke, army tales from her Uncle Bob, and the loud whispers and hot flushes of several Aunt Margarets in the kitchen scraping slivers of cabbage from colanders, swapping tales of hysterectomies and the things about Uncles they couldn't abide. In the living room one of Uncle Bob's dying Yorkshire terriers stretched itself beside the telephone table. To the left and above the dog, Mike Yarwood was making a hash of himself on the squarer, flatter TV screen. Jim, diminishing under the weight of the central heating, was tracing a journey between his first smile at Miriam and this anxiety of a late Saturday afternoon and Aunt Fuck's birthday celebration; sensing with cautious alarm the indecision of dinner – whether it would carry on with digestion or return the way it had come and have done with it. Miriam was all leg in her armchair, her cheeks flushed with an early brandy, her straw hat askew, watching without comment as Mike Yarwood began an impression which sounded like everyone between Gorbachev and Val Doonican at once. One of the Aunt Margarets was weeping because she'd been to school with the impressionist's second cousin.

That special Saturday. During the drive down Jim had seen a fat man throwing up bile on a grass verge beside the road and the image of it had stayed with him all day, reinforcing the sense of ill-health in himself. This, he now decided, had been the beginning of his condition. Uncle Bob had reached the part in his memoirs where he'd been forced to shoot a German soldier to save himself, and now reviewed his action in these peaceful years with a certain exhilaration and pride, rewarding himself with Hamlets whose effect was to make a dry, hot atmosphere drier and hotter but which lacked the sedative musical accompaniment remembered from television advertisements. Through the large window Jim watched blue tits swinging from a nut dispenser, as Uncle Bob's grandson Jeremy crawled across the lime carpet pretending to be a lion though he comprised ninety-nine per cent blancmange at that point, blobs of it still visible on his ginger mane. The lion was being tamed by consecutive relatives wielding phantom bentwood chairs. Miriam over there, curled up, a breath of fresh flesh and whispers . . . For the first time Jim was seeing her objectively. On the arm of her chair were pieces of a broken Bourbon biscuit; at the ends of her warm legs hung the pair of yellow Ali Akbar slippers lent to her by an aunt who didn't want high-heel marks on the Wilton and bought originally by Great Uncle Gilbert – formerly of the Foreign Office – who was now sleeping off the gin administered during dinner. He'd once had coffee with Keith Graves. That's how famous he was. Over dinner he had divided the world neatly into the British and the Bastards, and though the former were considerably outnumbered by the latter, it was the British people's job to keep the Bastards at bay with nuclear submarines and a strict immigration policy. In between his solitary toast to Enoch Powell and his journey to the bedroom in Uncle Bob's arms, he'd suggested that the heads of those awful Argentinians should have been displayed on the railings of Buckingham Palace as a deterrent to all other Bastards who'd had it too good for years. Such statements induced a tendency to wash up on the part of the Aunt Margarets each of whom, it was turning out, had been an Aunt

Margaret practically from the day they were born and each of whom came into the world with a talent for nosing out unsuitable gifts. The central heating meanwhile – sensing that several guests were still alive – overruled its own thermostat to procure a Saudi Arabian climate. Jim was watching Miriam's ankles and dreaming of the evening they'd had in bed with ropes and a bottle of Mateus Rosé. Uncle Bob, having illustrated the finer points of quickly dispatching those of German origin, was now miming the throwing of hand-grenades at whole bands of them coming over hills of Laura Ashley cushions. He'd ended up being presented with a medal by a Field Marshal McSomeone-or-other, which – if everyone didn't mind waiting just a moment – he'd go out to his car to fetch. He always brought it with him on family occasions just in case the subject came up. Pink with brandy and making Jim salivate (or was it the chicken?) Miriam fell asleep, and it was coming to him not only that he adored and disliked her but that she adored and disliked him: something in her skin which pulled, pushed him; something in her hands and the landscapes of thigh poking from her favourite skirt; the seduction destruction of her jade green eyes. He was thinking too of the number of times the word *Christopher* had come into her conversation of late. *Oh, you should see Christopher feeding the penguins. Christopher puts so much into his work. And by the way, Christopher and me are going to a slide show about the effects of global warming on Amazonian wildlife.* Jim lit a cigarette and watched as her head slid down the back of her chair, her skin a warm hazelnut colour from heat and over-eating, her tongue now and then sliding out to lubricate dry lips. Hadn't there been a lessening of something in their intimacy of late?

Moments of rope and wine but a lack of . . . Anyway, a lack. She'd laughed when he'd asked about this Christopher person. Laughed. And when she laughed at him it made him disbelieve the things his spirit believed, tearing him into two incompatible halves. Christopher had become most powerful through remaining unseen, merely a rumour of superiority. Damn it and smoke your cigarette. Miriam's power, even in her boneless sleep, was creating an impenetrable field. Aunt Harriet (who wasn't an Aunt at all but one of those extraneous relatives granted a title to mark long familiarity) was once again suffering a bout of flatulence, which the family had been asked to ignore since the poor soul was deaf and didn't realise, though early manifestations usually provoked some amusement from Uncle Bob, who'd been in the same training camp as Denis Norden. Aunt Harriet, so rumour suggested, had been knitting for seventy years, pausing only to marry and kill off a diminutive coalminer named Frank, who had passed-on as the only reasonable means of escape from pearl one tog two and oversalted oxtail soup. The news, which followed Yarwood, showed the Princess Royal visiting sick children and relegated the resignation of world governments to a thirty-second slot before the weather with John Kettley, who was chuckling over a vehemence of tightening isobars. Jim crossed the room to sit beside Miriam's chair, but her sleep had deepened and it seemed unlikely she would wake for a time. He had come to be near her fragrance and was now breathing it in, unable to decide whether he was fond of it or not. Knees together, her hand resting between them, a spot in the fold of her neck . . . Oh, an unspent rhapsody of knowing her inside out, the dangers of coming clean in the darkness of her mystery, and old remembered hymns of games among her limbs on afternoons always long ago, and here comes the salutation of an indiscriminate beast, an uncurling, a fattening-up, a reaching for that which would not please it at all. There are times he'd like to write her a letter about it, but words won't adequately express what's on his mind, Miriam on winter afternoons, blue trees through the window as she rolls deodorant under a raised arm, and for some reason she has to watch this ritual standing naked in front of a mirror, feet together, breath held to keep her abdomen in place. She loves to follow the line of her thighs with spread fingers or draw palms over soft breasts to swell them, her nipples pushed against the cold mirror as Jim lies on the bed with his third cigarette, ignoring, wanting her.

v

He passed over the breakfast he'd been offered, though the white plate holding sausages and scrambled egg had come with a message from Sister to do his best. He returned the plate with the explanation that his tummy was frail today – 'tummy' being the term she preferred. Making his way back to the side-room he saw Miranda in the office having tea and making elaborate gestures to a smiling colleague. He waved but she didn't see him. *Bollocks.* Some of the old men were moaning that the shrinking ward had brought them closer to the patient in the next bed. There was an unspoken principle that you could complain of the discomfort of having to listen to the sound of someone's insides dying without casting doubt on the character of the patient involved. A few of them nodded to Jim as he came by: old men with turkey necks gobbling breakfast. Back in his room he lit a cigarette. In all these years he hadn't got the hang of women, and it was as if time had conspired to prevent him getting the hang of them till they'd ceased wanting to get the hang of him. Now that he was at the tail-end of his life he realised he'd done nothing but fill the smallest of holes in the northern hemisphere. Didn't it seem that this matter of loving was less than insignificant at times?

While tidying the previous night, Miriam had placed the book Jeff had brought in for him on top of his magazine pile, making sure the borders of magazine visible beneath the book were equal on all sides. He wasn't sure whether he enjoyed this trait of hers or not. Nor, indeed, whether he was any more than tolerant of *The Blue Kiosk*. As yet he could extract no suggestion of plot; the characters were spectral at best; and as for the haphazard structure, it did nothing but carry him towards sleep as inevitably as his night-time medication. On the other hand, like being alive itself, it did help pass the time.

A child (Jim read) comes awake thrashing the surface of the pond, waiting for Oswald to turn up. The world then just an apple tree with a rope dangling from it on which I could swing across the ocean drunk with the perfume of honeysuckle. On a bank of dock and dandelion I waggled my baseball boots and ate a biscuit. Over the wall I could see the upper third of Bumper Daniels searching his scrapyard for children crouched among the stingers, rusting cars or piles of gravel. I was squashed, unforgiven, full of unwritten poems, watching moorhens divide green shadows under the low tunnel which carried the stream from here, beneath both scrapyard and road, to a wasteground beyond.

Soon Oswald swept into the pub yard on his bike and came to a halt with a skid. Following an unspoken routine we left the yard with our sticks, crossed the empty road and entered the acre of mudbumps left years before by over-ambitious builders who'd suddenly gone out of business. Here were dwarfs, dead children, Princes of Darkness and – several times a day – the tall, oily figure of Bumper Daniels. He'd extended his search for the wicked, parting undergrowth with a stick, spitting phlegm to one side as he passed the homosexuals' house, fairy buggers, all the women in the world and they had to go snogging in a cottage with clematis round the door and a blue-rinsed poodle in the front yard yapping politely at passers-by.

Further on, we passed Jane's house. If the number one on his list – Laurinda Hallpike – didn't marry Oswald, then Jane was to be his second choice. She often called him a prat from an upstairs window and threw blotting-paper soaked in ink to make him blue about the nose. Oswald was a colourless, lean, ugly person to have around and – as Jane called out one day – no one would touch him with a fifty-foot stick, and if they did it would only be to test him for pustules. Jane had recently found the word in her dictionary. At which point Oswald went crimson and ran ahead to the wooden bridge, his nose never reaching a state of clearance despite packets of Handy Andys by day and snips of Karvol at night. I continued pushing him into a bush if a suitable one passed by and Oswald, bless him, climbed out each time with a grin about his chops. On to the sweet shop by the printing works, where we bought a couple of liquorice pipes, the fire in their bowls represented by a scattering of hundreds of thousands. Oswald settled for the smaller of the pipes, though there wasn't much difference. We spent a long droning afternoon among the chestnuts throwing gravel at Colonel Anderson's favourite grey before going to our den in the copse to smoke Senior Service stolen from the pub bar. Later we compared sizes of more intimate pipes. Oswald's was the smaller of course, being a Roman Catholic one. Women, I said, don't have pubic hair unless they've been kissed between the legs. Oswald didn't believe this till we'd got hold of some pictures. We studied them another afternoon under the old corrugated lean-to in the pub yard where the empties were kept. In summer every wasp for miles came to hum aborigine melodies in their sticky necks. At weekends we were paid threepence for every dozen we could swat.

A tap on the door announced Mr Cook, who edged into the room, strode to the window, clapped his hands, then briskly rubbed them together as if to warm himself. For a consultant he was casually dressed – a blue corduroy coat and trousers – though his status was affirmed by a large grey dickie-bow at the crest of his white shirt. Rumours from Doris that Cook was a heavy drinker and a bit of a lad were borne out by a faint smell of stale whisky and betrayal following in his wake. He was short, barely head and shoulders above the windowsill, like a withered child, and yet he had the pink complexion and stylish silvered hair of one who lives well. His stature made a silent joke of his profession and Jim had sensed – the few times he'd met him – a need to compensate for this. We can ignore the short, but they rarely escape the discomfort of a context common to them all.

'Well Jim,' he said without turning round, 'how are you doing today?'

Jim put *The Blue Kiosk* to one side. 'Up and down, Mr Cook. Up and down.'

'And what about your state of mind? How's your *thinking*?'

Jim took his time over this, re-arranging his dressing-gown and patting the pillow. 'Fairly good on the whole. I've been quite pleased with myself.'

Turning away from the window, Cook studied Jim's observation chart and said, apparently to himself, 'Good man, good man.' He returned to the window, looked out and took a deep breath, finally exhaling with, 'Splendid day, isn't it? Walking up the road just now I could have sworn I smelt fresh pickles. You know, the tang hanging round a kitchen when they've been bottled the night before. Took me right back. A sniff of pickle means Autumn to me, Jim. Autumn has quite a bad reputation. I mean, it's neither one thing nor the other, but I quite like it. How about you?'

Jim shrugged. 'It's all right, I suppose. The leaves can be nice.'

The consultant rocked onto his brushed suede toes. 'And this Autumn is a particularly significant one for you, isn't it?'

Sensing this question was rhetorical, Jim simply waggled his bottom jaw and stretched his toes.

'And I suppose its most outworn and romantic metaphors are continually unravelling for you, eh? Decay, demise, the end of loving – all that kind of thing.'

'Yes, there are times when I've –.'

'I understand Jim. I understand. That's my job, to understand.'

Coughing politely, he swivelled round and sat in the chair by Jim's bed, making a rest for his chin with linked hands. He was watching the patient closely and absently swinging a pair of feet which didn't quite reach the floor.

'The nurse was telling me you might have some good news, Mr Cook.'

Cook smiled, lowed the triangle of forearms onto his knees and leaned forwards.

'Well, Jim, I expect you've heard all kinds of stories in the press and on TV about how hard-pressed we medical people are these days, what with lack of money, staff shortages and all that. I can tell you now, it's all true. In fact the situation's even worse than they let on. Take me, for example. Once upon a time my day was made up of operations and one-to-one contact with the patient. Now I find myself sitting behind a desk more than I think reasonable and from minute to minute I'm having to weigh up priorities. God – if you like – makes detrimental financial decisions and leaves us disciples to implement them. Grape?'

'No thank you.'

'Do you mind if . . . '

'No. You go ahead.'

Cook unplucked a pair of the dusty purple spheres from the bunch in the fruitbowl and popped them into his mouth. 'This is the next best thing to having them fermented,' he said. For a moment or two the silence was used up by sounds of mastication and the movement of his epiglotis as he swallowed the pulp. Jim looked over the corduroy shoulder to the window, but looked back quickly when Cook said with much emphasis: 'I know an old woman, Jim.'

'Oh, that's . . . '

'An old woman who's suffering *greatly*. And do you know why she's suffering greatly?' He plucked a third grape and rolled it in the cupped palm of his left hand. 'I'll tell you why. She's been waiting over nine months for a reasonably straightforward operation which I'm confident would bring her a complete recovery. Over nine months. Tragic, isn't it? An innocent old woman has to suffer because of what are simply logistical problems. We haven't the space for her, as you can see. Don't you find that awful? Worse than awful, inhuman. I dare say you wouldn't enjoy telling her nothing could be done till next summer.'

Jim was keeping his head still, fearing Cook's possible misinterpretation of a nod or shake at the wrong moment.

'If I had a bed we could haul in the old soul and get her fixed up in no time. Some of my colleagues think the young should take priority over the elderly, but I believe these people have a right to the best of care. Look at all they've been through. If you can't have a decent old age, then what's the point? I don't mind telling you, the whole thing upsets me a great deal.'

Changing his mind, Jim reached for a grape himself and engaged – as he always did – in the art of unpeeling it in his mouth. This feat always brought home to him the subtlety and skill of the human body. Cook meanwhile was fumbling for Jim's hand. He found it, but squeezed for no longer than would have been proper.

'Now you and I, Jim, we've always been straightforward with one another, haven't we? In fact you've told me yourself you don't like secrecy and I go along with that. You know you don't have long to go and I've admired the pluck you've shown in living with that fact. Others I could name would have become ill with worry. But you Jim? No sign of it.'

Jim's cheeks coloured. 'Thank you.'

'Then again, I don't care what anyone says, it can't be good for you not knowing *when* it's going to happen. I mean, it could be in a month. Could be in a couple of days. Who *does* know? Who does? I'll bet you're constantly on the look-out for signals.'

The chewed grape was making its way reluctantly down Jim's oesophagus. As soon as it had arrived at his stomach he looked deep into Cook's eyes.

'I'm getting your drift,' he said. 'You'd like this room for the old lady and you're figuring you might as well send me home to die.'

Cook shook his head. 'Where would be the sense in that, Jim? I'm sure your wife has enough on her plate at the moment without having to look after you as well. Don't get me wrong, I'm all for community care, but in this case . . .'

Jim laughed. 'What are you going to do then? Put me down or something?'

Cook reached for Jim's hand a second time. 'I prefer to use the term voluntary euthanasia. Believe me, we have an Aladdin's cave of suitable drugs which can make anything seem a pleasant experience. And I have a highly recommended cocktail in mind.'

Sensing Cook wouldn't make a fuss, Jim pulled away his hand and reached for a cigarette. It was difficult to light.

'And to my way of thinking, the discomfort of knowing you're going to pass on at some indeterminate time could easily be dispelled by choosing a firm appointment for your departure. We could, for example, make it Thursday afternoon.'

Jim spat a strand of tobacco from his tongue. 'What time?'

'I was thinking of four o'clock. Just before tea. The trick of it is to begin a new drug regime several hours beforehand so by the time your appointment comes you won't mind one way or the other. And I want you to know, Jim, that I've thought this through very carefully, for *your* sake as well as for Mrs Clipthorne's.'

Jim exhaled. 'Thank you.'

'And let's be realists, Jim. Left to its own devices death can be a messy business. You wouldn't like it. Who's to say it would happen in the right place in the right conditions with the right people around you? At least with my plan everything's taken care of and you can go knowing Mrs Clipthorne will always be grateful to you and – providing you have some decent internal organs left – by late Thursday night there could be three or four other people owing their very lives to you. Not many chaps can say *that*, can they?'

Not till he had lit another cigarette did Jim realise the first was still smouldering in the saucer. Smiling, Cook stubbed it out.

'I haven't told your wife of our little plan yet.' He patted Jim's knee. 'I thought it would be best coming from you. From what I've seen of you I'm sure your resilience and *joie de vivre* will be a source of great strength to her later on. And I'm so terribly glad you and I have seen eye to eye on this. Terribly glad.'

He raised a curled fist as if to cough but used it to half-shield a yawn, then took Jim's hand once more, shaking it with some ferocity. Having climbed to his feet, he stretched himself till the tips of his fingers – despite his child's stature – brushed the strip-light.

'Now, I'm sure you have a few things to think over so I'm going to run along. I'll be with you around three on Thursday and we'll take it from there.'

Jim smiled. 'You'd better ring Mrs Fucking Clipthorne in the meantime then.'

* * *

As soon as the short-arsed Cook bastard had gone, Jim rolled out of bed and settled in the rexine-covered chair, listening to the hum of the ward beyond his room, smoking more cigarettes, wondering when Miranda or anyone would come back. He was heavy, as if his mass would eventually pull him through the floor. Like the short chorus of a repetitive opera by a punk rocker, the word *Bollocks* was running through his head. He quietened it temporarily by thinking back to not so long ago when each day he'd woken up in the camp bed expecting his exhaustion to have fled in the night, only to find that by the time he'd made Miriam's coffee it was with him once more. And there was all that energy he'd wasted in the belief his ailments were connected to a cool discontent with the ways of home and modern living – an incompatibility with furniture warehouses, non-perishable plastic wrappings and sick food originating from lambs with Anthrax poisoning. Miriam had her moments of displeasure too, but these had usually been directed at the workings of kitchen appliances. Where Jim's gloom, when spoken, was global, Miriam's would seem to be based on the uneven performance of her Kenwood Chef. Then there was Uncle Tobias – or 'Buggerface' as he'd come to be known – filling the house with the clatter of his zimmer frame and an unbroken resentment that his own incapacity had come along to prevent the completion of his thesis. He'd been disowned by other members of the family long before on the basis of occasional voluntary incontinence and a habit he'd developed in disability which involved pushing his hand up passing women's skirts. This latter behaviour he'd blamed on sudden contractions consistent with Huntington's Chorea, which he didn't have. And he wouldn't yield to sleep at night till the withered thesis had been tucked beneath his pillow, though its bulk must have been the cause of great discomfort to him. It had been his sole preoccupation – a philosophical treatise on *The Nature of Life*, each chapter involving a discussion of one of its more problematical areas. In some remaining corner of coherence Buggerface held on to the idea that its sound reasoning might seep through the pillow overnight and facilitate a complete recovery. Prior to his cerebral accident he had indeed been one of the few philosophical academic characters in Jim's immediate family; yet he'd also become the butt of many cruel jokes, having put study as a priority over long-term relationships with women. For at least twenty years, as far as Jim could remember, Buggerface had excused himself from most family gatherings on the grounds that he was 'working on his thesis'. In those early days, as a rather handsome bewhiskered old gentleman not unlike Cap'n Birdseye, he often confessed to Jim that his ultimate aim – that is, his hope for the last chapter – was to arrive at a short coherent and easy to follow solution to living itself: a profound aphorism at which readers might nod and say to themselves, 'Aha! Why didn't I think of that?' He had been working on the last but one chapter the morning of the stroke which marked the end of his ordered meanderings, as if he'd become the embodiment of the impossibility of that proposed summing-up. Despite this there were almost a thousand pages, covering subjects which ranged from *The Problem Of Aunts At Christmas* to the need for a new design for bends in sink waste-pipes to prevent the necessity of removing by hand the mixture of hair, bacon rind and old spaghetti invariably found there. Of course, like most folk of a philosophical bent, his personal life had been less than successful, though some years earlier he had managed an on-off friendship with a crinkled woman from out of town, whose unpredictable character was no doubt the inspiration for the sub-chapter *Why Are Girls Such Buggers?* In his time he'd acquired a reputation as a difficult bloke, a rebel, one who found it virtually impossible to engage in any normal social activity since an analysis of such activity during the course of his work had led him to the conclusion that it was all 'hogwash'. The gradual broadening of the concept of hogwash led him to abandon the observance of Bank Holidays and refuse to entertain bottles of Domestos in his bathroom. He would no longer wear suits, have injections at the dentist, put his correct date of birth on census forms, or quash the instinct to pin open letters to the current Mayor on the front gate – letters which protested at the expense of large cloaks, red-faced men in claret-coloured suits and horses with feathered nose-bands. Perhaps it was an early symptom of cerebral dysfunctioning which made him roar with laughter whenever the Pope appeared on TV and refuse to pay his National Insurance Contributions during periods of self-employment – a rebellion which eventually led to his having to be cared for by relatives in this latter part of his life and to borrow the occasional pound for 'sure things' at Lingfield. Only those who'd read the thesis could reason why he'd throw up his arms and shout 'Oh, foxgloves!' when his chosen horse was last past the post: chapter eighteen comprised a simple though lengthy dictionary of alternatives to bad language or, as he called it, 'cursing'. Why not, he reasoned, replace such harsh, unromantic words with those of a floral kind. Hence, 'I'll have your cowslips for garters', and (on the occasion perhaps of striking one's fingers with a hammer) 'Oh bluebell me.'

And the point of it all – as the author may have said – is that morals can be hogwash too, some primeval finger wagging at us so we don't live all we might, putting aside dark parts, such as kissing where thigh is softest in strangers, becoming moist sometimes at a line of leg in shorts, denim tugged towards insoluble realms, strands of hair, a sweep of underthighs, and dark secrets in an unstitched cave, the prowess coming, if this is prowess, after months of weakness, yet it's everything, we realise. If we own our prowess, then everything will be well; pain strikes only when we are no longer fond of ourselves, when prowess flees and we're stuck for something to love, other than love itself or God, and some way to express it. A favourite moment would be nothing to do with him or her but something rumouring beneath the inconceivable, music playing there, rhythm endlessly renewing itself. These may be the hogwashes of the patient made noble, considerate of spirit not flesh, which could explain those lonely corners, yet words are such poor substitutes for truth, which like an owl must fly in twilight against a flash of corn. An owl flying on the crest of moonlit unconnections.

vi

'You'll have to smoke less, Jim. The alarm will be going off if you're not careful.'

Turning round, he was in time to catch Miranda closing the door with a thrust of her bottom. In her hands was a tray with a plate of scrambled eggs, sausages and two slices of bread, all of which glistened under the fluorescent light.

'I've sent the damn breakfast back once.'

'Don't blame me. It was Sister.' Indicating he should lie on the bed, she swung his mahogany patterned breakfast trolley into position, then placed the tray before him. To pass time, he cut the sausages in two. Both of them exuded a trickle of watery grease which ran to the edges of his plate and in time congealed into a thin paste. The extremities of each sausage were capped with a black crust, and the pink flesh within was releasing an aroma of farmyards, of undercooked pig. He fancied he could hear them squeal. The scrambled egg was dry and springy, and had gone a dull yellow with flecks of grey. Miranda folded her arms and watched as he choreographed the various components around the plate with the tip of his knife.

'He's told us the news.'

Jim glanced at the faint dome of her belly. 'What news? Who?'

'Mr Cook. He called us into the office and counselled us. That's why Sister's sent breakfast. You should look at it as an unprecedented gesture of goodwill from the old crow.'

'Tell her the spirit's willing but the duodenum's weak.'

'Come on. Tuck in.' Taking the fork from his left hand she leaned close to him, scooped up a few pellets of scrambled egg and offered it to his mouth. A smell of sweat and shower gel reached the pit of his stomach while his eyes fixed on the fork, which was shaking slightly. 'If you had a bit I'm sure you'd feel better.' Obediently, Jim opened wide, going cross-eyed as Miranda slipped the fork into his mouth. He closed his lips as she withdrew, swallowing immediately to avoid the taste. She inhaled with pleasure. 'There. That wasn't so bad, was it?'

'No. But I'd rather not have the rest if you don't mind.'

The fork clattered to the plate. She sat on the edge of his bed. Her apple bottom fattened. Jim pushed the trolley away and fiddled with his fingers. 'Will you be there? On Thursday, I mean?'

She was busy tucking a strand of hair back into her cap. 'Depends. My shift ends at three officially, but if we're busy I'm sometimes here at four. Whatever happens, I don't want to be hanging around too long because I'm going to the theatre in the evening.'

Jim withdrew his hand from the cigarette packet following a shake of her head. 'And what are you going to see?'

'*The Tempest.*'

'What time does it start?'

'Half past seven I think. Why?'

He laughed. 'No reason.' His eyes were drawn to the tightness of her lilac uniform where her thighs had broadened from sitting down. He followed the line of her hips to her naked forearms and the mist of dark hair upon them, then looked at the fob-watch on her chest and listened to its ticking. Catching his hands in hers, she lay them against her leg.

'Now, is there anything you'd like? You know, things which would make you more comfortable. Can't promise the earth, of course, but say the word and we'll certainly do what we can.'

Her hands were cool. 'Nothing springs to mind this minute,' he said.

Letting go of him, she reached for *The Blue Kiosk* and stared at the cover, which showed a pair of young boys in silhouette against the moon with a lace of black willow leaves in the foreground. 'What's this like then?'

'Oh, I haven't made up my mind yet. I've not long started it. The blurb says you can read any bit of it in any order you like. It's chronologically formless, you know the kind of thing.'

She threw it back onto the pile of magazines, sniffed, and repositioned herself, supporting her body with a splayed hand which rested against his leg just below the hem of his dressing-gown where it was naked and uninteresting. He regretted his oversized slippers, the ones Miriam had bought him accidentally for Christmas. On the box it had classified their colour as 'Afghanistan Grey'. They'd been in a sale, and by the look of them they were probably the last pair of slippers on earth not to have been snapped up till Miriam chanced by. In view of their looseness, they slapped the floor wherever he walked, only to be caught up at a much later date by his descending heels. The hair on his shins was scruffy. And, in his position, his feet and slippers had a tendency to splay, an attitude he couldn't imagine anyone loving. His body went well till it entered those realms beneath the knees, where it was as if his creator had run out of patience. The skin at his ankles was blue and a little puffed up. Miranda had turned her attention to them, though he guessed there were daydreams playing over their unwelcome surfaces. Suddenly she stood, and, having yawned, tapped her fingers against the window.

'In many ways I envy you,' she said. 'The earth's a pretty scary place to be. I mean, you see them on the news every day, people crying out for freedom, but they're so gloomy about it, as if freedom's going to be a dangerous thing.' Jim was watching her backside, well-stocked legs and ubiquitous brown shoes with tan heels. A moment of sunlight surrounded her, throwing her shadow against the opposite wall . . . and the town was an unthinkable place, extremes of the beautiful tempered by devils. This time of year it was wet and in decay, melancholy yet rapturous too, filled with old memories and yesterday's lyrics, a shrinking, irregular refuge not fit for seagulls, occasionally throwing up dark grins from old men tucked under cemetery walls.

'Everything's dangerous,' he said.

Miranda turned round and smiled, as if she'd caught herself acting out of character. 'I'd better not stand here all day talking. She'll be after me. What about this breakfast?'

Jim looked at it to see if it had become any more appetising. 'Sorry.'

'Don't worry I'll throw it away before she has a chance to look.'

Collecting the tray she pecked Jim on the forehead and hurried out. For a while he lay on his back trying to objectify the twisting in his guts. Then, having failed in this, he picked a place at random from *The Blue Kiosk*, though with no enthusiasm or peace of mind.

Oswald would lounge in class watching some girl across the aisle with moons in his eyes, her ignorance of him indicating to his sense of optimism her true feelings. As a potential lover he was ever ready to interpret reaction or lack of reaction as complimentary to himself. He would confide in me that where his gazing was met with avoidance on the girl's part, she was merely fooling herself, boiling with a passion she was unable to acknowledge. Miss Purvis would scratch sums on the blackboard in mixtures of dust and fingernails. She disliked children, and loved beating them with a leather-bound volume called *Bernstein's Imperial Rome* whenever the occasion merited. Over the course of a term merited occasions would become indistinguishable from those of an unmerited nature, so it came to pass we feared a swiping from the volume for the crime of being nothing more than ourselves. She hated swinging legs, fingers in ears, hair in plaits, children who were sick and – probably most of all – Oswald's nose, an extremity towards which she didn't once show a moment's forgiveness. The fact of his being alive at all proved a source of great irritation to her, his trousers rushing towards *Bernstein's Imperial Rome* two or three times a week. She disliked, too, those children with the audacity to be small and it became her practice to thrash them till they learned not to be small in future. To maximise opportunities for a good thrashing she also included being big on her list of misbehaviours and – supposing by some miracle a child contrived overnight to be small no longer – he then risked a beating if he'd overdone it slightly.

We imagined that beyond the classrooms lay places of great freedom and through the far window we could see the spring town smoking like an ancient professor reviewing wisdoms. Each day we walked to school past the corrugated tin shed where a deaf and dumb man mended watches, and the community convent through whose windows Oswald once saw a nun in a state of seminudity. He made an entry about it that night in his diary, though he used code to spare his mother who had developed the habit of rooting through his fantasies. Going to school was always a hazard, since a rat called Freddy Something loved to slink in alleys and beat the spleens of passing juniors. He'd only keep his fists in his pockets if we gave him a packet of Rowntree's Fruit Pastilles, which we couldn't always afford. Sixpence pocket-money for the week and no guts to ask your mum for more. Afraid of living so soon, and the town hadn't even acknowledged the threat of terrorist states. We wouldn't have been surprised to have seen cannon on the hill in readiness for an invasion of Spaniards – a possibility guarded against by the Town Mayor, who also ran the three-piece suite shop but spent most of his time rocking on his heels in the doorway because no one bought three-piece suites in our town. As he rocked, his status as Mayor would bubble to the surface, making it essential for him to watch the street, ears pricked for the first rumble of attack even as he stepped into the road to direct old men's Ford Populars round the corner into Rag Street. He had been picked as Mayor because he was the one wearing brushed suede shoes, checked shirt and a professorial jacket with leather patches and a spotted hanky. We waved to him as we passed each day, Oswald with a Cadbury's Finger sideways in his mouth, and I'd be hating my friend for his emaciated silliness, his unsnagged jacket, that nose burnished with tireless flannels till daylight sadly emphasised its volume. If you met Oswald on the street he'd giggle greetings at you, his nostrils widening and narrowing in rapid succession. That's how you knew when he was pleased to see you. At the same time, a throwing-back of the head would ruin the McCartney fringe and give you an unwelcome view of his tonsils.

The summer holidays came and Oswald still featured heavily, since this was his time. The earth was baking, covered in chips of bleached limestone and brittle yellow grass. The farm lay in ripples at the end of a long track. Strolling between the two of us this particular day was Laurinda Hallpike in a simple summer dress strewn with forget-me-nots. Oswald took every opportunity to describe my defects in case her affections should fall the wrong way. We were taking her home. To one side a dark green wood splashed into the valley. She was the countryside, smelling of cow's milk and ripening corn, her legs tanned and scratched, her shoes once white but now scuffed into a pattern of greys and blacks. Her brother George attended a special school because he was someone who'd soon be described as a person with learning difficulties, though in those days it meant he'd think nothing of executing blackbirds or tossing pieces of drystone wall at sheep.

Oswald was saying something like: 'Hey! Let's go down the barn s'afto.'

Laurinda, reddening about the throat, reminded him her father didn't allow kids in his barns. Oswald kicked a piece of limestone. He'd got it into his head – despite weekly Mass – that Girl plus Straw equals Something, and his project for the summer was to find out what. I was the scruffy one thinking through lines from *Under Milk Wood*, girls either loving me or making jokes about my haircut.

'What about the pool then?'

'Too far,' said Laurinda. 'Besides, George is coming home later and mum wants me to play with him.'

Oswald was trailing his fingers through the hazel leaves which drooped over the track, his knees dangling from a pair of Trutex shorts. However brown they became, his knees hinted of soft Catholic thighs just above. I was poking my hands into the pockets of my favourite jeans. Now, let me see: something about the dark and a constable with a beef-red huff . . . But the undergarments of this countryside hadn't sinned enough to stage the antics of memory. This was a cruel place in summer: cracks in the soil if the rains stayed away; old labourers sitting in the corners of gnat-heavy fields swigging cider; and the prospect of George coming home in secret to jump from the bushes at us with a rock in each hand.

'Well then,' Oswald said, 'what about tomorrow? Do you fancy coming out tomorrow?'

'Might. Might not,' said Laurinda Hallpike as Oswald reared to look down the front of her forget-me-not dress. Farm girls always had swellings first, and Oswald would dream of their eventual shape and texture through many mouth-watering years – till he became a priest and sacrificed his opportunity.

'Tell you what,' he was saying, 'we'll wait for you just

here at eleven tomorrow. Come if you can. We'll hide in the trees and call if we see you first. What d'you reckon?'

'Triffic,' said Laurinda Hallpike.

Oswald snorted. I knew Laurinda was already making jokes about his nose to her friends and for a moment I was hurt for him. We'd stopped at the gate and were watching as she clambered over, waved, and ran towards the farmhouse. Oswald giggled to himself.

'I saw her knickers,' he said.

'Great.'

'And guess what? I met Ronnie up the street yesterday and he said she'd take them off for a tanner.'

'If it's ever going to mean anything,' I said, 'she'll take them off for nothing.'

He snorted once more. 'Yeah? D'you think so? Hey that would be Fan tastic.'

'You are daft.'

He was laughing half-heartedly, as if he wasn't sure of my commitment to the idea. His nose issued twangs of mucus and wonderment. So many flaws gathered into a single person, which was the reason for his ending up a man of the cloth with a love of gin, God, and those pastel-coloured churches, while I was a mix of lunacies, a child thinking of himself as not-a-child, already finding more in corners than met the eye, something unsimple harking back to Captain Cat, rhymes from upstairs windows and songs from unmet girls in Wurlitzer skirts.

vii

Having dressed and written a note to say where he was going, Jim made his way along the main corridor, moved slowly down the flight of steps and let himself into the hospital garden – a colourless sanctuary for patients and their visitors, with views into Museum Street at a level with the lime trees whose leaves had blown onto the grey concrete paving and gathered round small, unlit shrubs. Patients from the psychiatric wing had congregated at the far end to smoke cigarettes and swap misfortunes. Choosing a bench nearest the white railing, Jim settled down to that tang of pickle, the warmth of rainbow pedestrians, wet leaves, and Laura – extracts of her busy white hand and champagne hair, the folds of her cobweb skirt. Above him, a scrubbed blue sky, meringues of white cloud and, in the air itself, a treacle-coloured sunlight hanging over top-floor windows.

He remembered coming over the crest of a gravelled track to see such a sunlight melting through oak trees, leaving traces of itself against the cracked skin of their branches. Laura had a way of laughing like water in a hidden brook. Her name was the secret tale of an afternoon almost spent, and though both knew they were fooling themselves they kept the secret anyway, as something to unwrap in speechless dark. Her legs soft with hair catching the sticky sun, and there were dandelion seeds floating in the light wind. He could have skipped like an imp in spring, his tomfoolery interwoven with silence, then a cascade of oak roots where the soil had been washed away. She posed him for a photograph which was ruined by a man coming by wrapped in a white tuba. I mend mistakes as I go along, before the number of them overwhelms me. Such afternoons have their own perfume: leaves, toadstools, moistures from the creases in her thighs. She was reminding him of someone, though every time he tried to think it through she teased him and ruined it. He made a speech against falling which lasted maybe half an hour, only to be disrupted by her supposition that a fuck was therefore out of the question. Nothing like an honest woman to illuminate those uptight boyhoods. 'Yes, it is,' he said. Over the ridge where the trees thinned they spotted a rocky outcrop, climbed as high as they could and waited there, her rib glimpsed through loops of crimson T-shirt as she lay back against the mattress of cliff grass, her eyes lit by something inside he hadn't seen before. Later, in the café, she had bread-and-butter pudding topped with ice-cream. Everyone but Laura was in fucking knots, yet they gave the condition fine names. On the next table a couple were arguing about Germany. The woman was saying: 'Perhaps someone should now build a division, a wall or something.' Pages of narrative reduced to a few grey words. There were old women with cappucino lips and black, scallop-shaped handbags. Engraved spoonfuls of pudding travelled to Laura's mouth leaving traces of ice-cream in its corners, which – in her car later – he licked away. Dvořák playing on the car radio, Jim kissing her light brown knee, then a belly offered by a raising of her T-shirt, while outside the footpath became a black thread winding towards the sun. Her mouth was the moist opening into a second world. Between unfinished goodbyes he was smoking cigarettes, idling through stations on the radio, resting his elbow on the opened window. Downwind a collie snapped at a tethered goat and weekend schoolgirls were slipping on the grass as they played round the cliff. Sometimes pleats fluttered upwards to the whistles of friends or men with cans of Yorkshire Bitter or the sonnets of bald men with spectacles and carved wives carrying between them bags holding the secrets of thirty years: hairnets, tubes of Giovanni lipstick, ozone-friendly perfume sprays, the telephone numbers of chimney sweeps on printed cards. 'Won't you let me peck you just here,' Laura was saying, and though he wanted her to gobble him there more than anywhere he said she'd better not because of conflagration, consequences and the sideways glances of priests out for a stroll, poets shaking out the blood from their hands, and children geeing up invisible horses. 'Between the world and me, one of us is nuts,' she said.

Someone was calling his name. He twisted on the bench to see Jeff heading for him, his hand held up and his mouth wide as a new moon.

'Thought you'd hopped it for a moment,' he was saying. Jim shuffled sideways to make room as Jeff grasped the creases in his trousers and sat down.

'You should have told them you were coming out here. They went mad till they saw your note.'

'I really needed some fresh air.'

'Are you warm enough? You should have brought your coat.' He tickled the side of his nose. 'Come on then. How are you? What's the score?'

'One nil to the grim reaper.'

It was well known that Jeff couldn't handle personification and, as usually happened when forced into it, he looked down with a scowl. Jim lit a cigarette.

'We don't have to talk about me, Jeff. How are things at work?'

Jeff recovered. 'Oh, you know. Jacobson getting on everyone's nerves. Generally frantic. You'll be pleased to hear we've had quite a time of it taking on your part of the work.'

Allowing the cigarette to rest in his lips, Jim had folded his arms and was squinting against the rising smoke as Jeff traced invisible patterns on the concrete with the tip of his left shoe. At work, Jim had always wanted to take a razor to his friend's sideburns which, through neglect and an immoral adherence to the sixties, were in danger of becoming eccentric; but today, in crucifixion mood, he was thinking maybe it would be more Christian to turn a blind eye – give those leading whiskers an opportunity to liaise in the vicinity of the chin. This might even add credence to those crests and troughs of ginger hair which, being similar in texture to candyfloss, were at the mercy of the slightest breath of wind. Lodged on his nose were the familiar oblong lenses with diagonally cut corners somehow held in place by frail, gold-plated frames, the wings of which lost themselves on their approach to Jeff's ears. Jim was figuring it was a good thing ears and noses had evolved in such convenient positions. The human frame was altogether remarkable in its suitability for invention.

Something troubled Jeff. He had thrown his hands behind his head and was looking into the sky.

'It's no good, Jim. It's terrible trying to talk normally with you when we're in such different circumstances. Here am I, just inches from you, and even though we've been best mates for a while I'm trying not to look glad I'm not you. Isn't that awful? When I came through that door I decided I was going to be straight with you. I don't want to end up like one of those people who won't refer to what's going on. I know you wouldn't respect me if I did. Didn't.'

'Don't worry all the time, Jeff. Just tell me about work.'

Jeff pressed his friend's hand. Jim watched the pressed area as Jeff took a deep breath and threw his head forward.

'Well, as I said, old Jacobson's much the same. We reckon he's gone back on the booze. Remember how puffed his eyelids used to be? Well, he can hardly see out of them now. And he's nastier than ever, as if that wasn't nasty enough. Always making Jenny cry. As you might guess, she's still looking for Mr Right, only she's not so bothered about him being British. She's widened the field to include EC countries. Getting ready for 1992, she says. And Joe – he's as mad as ever. Keeps getting into trouble with Jacobson for being late and stinking out the office with those egg and anchovy sandwiches.'

Jim was stubbing out his cigarette. 'It's just occurred to me everyone in the office has a name beginning with J.'

Jeff chewed his gum for a moment then jerked his chin upwards, laughing. 'Good grief, you're right, Jim. Why haven't we remarked on it before?'

Beyond Jeff's shoulder, towards the back of the garden, a patient in allsorts pyjamas was trying a handstand. Jim turned away and squeezed the bridge of his nose.

'Of course, we're cheating a bit,' he said. 'We've manipulated the information to give verification to an underlying trend. You see, if we called Jacobson by his Christian name then the J factor, though still predominant, wouldn't absolutely apply.'

'D for Danny you mean? Yes, I can see that. You're saying we've called him Jacobson not only because we don't like him enough to call him Danny but also to make the J trend absolute.'

'I think so,' said Jim, holding out his pack of cigarettes to Jeff, who shook his head.

'Boy, Jim, you get to me sometimes. I doubt if all that would have occurred to me in a month of

Sundays if you hadn't been around to point it out. I do admire you for being clear-headed enough to spot these things. If I was . . . well, you know, if I was in your position I don't think I'd be giving predominant initial letters a second thought.'

The sun's rays were warm against Jim's skin. Momentarily he was brought to a state of peace by a series of random images: a mother lifting a small child for games at the edge of the sea; squirrels jumping through a canopy of oak trees; the moon and Venus in a cold sky Laura once compared to a Christmas card; horses on white November mornings; children throwing sticks into conker trees. As if the solemnity of this moment had infected Jeff, he too relaxed, interlocking his fingers and resting them between his knees.

'Jim, I haven't dared ask you before but . . . what's it like?'

'What's what like?'

'You know.'

Jim straightened. 'It's hard to say exactly. One minute the idea's beautiful, the next it's an awesome thing scaring me silly but making me sit tight like a child on a ghost train. I find myself wanting to hurry towards it and run away at the same time. Of course, you can't really share someone's feelings about it till you're on the brink yourself, and anyway, it's always an individual thing in the end. I've cried over it – of course I have. Fought against it even. But still there's some mystical aspect of it which attracts me. The adventure of going into the unknown, I suppose.'

Jeff was blushing. 'And do you think it's best with the woman on top or what?'

A quarter to something, the peal of church bells was filling the garden. Jim nodded, though not in reply to Jeff's question particularly.

Jeff cleared his throat. 'Look, I'm sorry. I seem to have strayed onto the subject of me again. To be honest I'm thinking of Mei Lee.'

'You don't need to apologise Jeff. I know how you feel about her and it must be driving you potty after all this time. Haven't you made any progress at all?'

Jeff dragged his fingers down the side of his face. 'Not a lot. I said hello to her this morning and she smiled at me, but then she smiles at everyone, doesn't she? That's her job after all. Smiling. Every night I dream up speeches, but when I get to the office it's all I can do to open my mouth. I'm beginning to think I'm not the sort of person to carry this off, Jim. When I see her there at the desk and she looks up I sort of die inside – sorry . . . Then Jacobson's been winding me up. Reckons he's been reading about women of her nationality and keeps telling me that if I went out with her I'd have to go abroad to meet her parents and take part in dancing rituals round a fire. And if you get on well with the parents everything's great, but once you're married you only have to stray even slightly and the relatives come over to chop your hand off. I think that's what he said – hand. I never know how seriously to take Jacobson. I mean, I wouldn't want to go to Vietnam even for the weekend. But the point is, I think I love her and I've been dreaming of asking her to marry me. Her eyes started it. Tell me I'm being ridiculous, Jim.'

'Not a bit of it. You stick to your guns. She's probably waiting for you to make the first move.'

Jeff's eyes narrowed. 'Thanks, Jim, but you're just trying to cheer me up. I'm not cut out for it. Women are a complete mystery to me. You never know what they're thinking, do you? And even if you do manage to wheedle it out of them it's not much help. And I'm not saying I believe Jacobson, but there are bound to be differences, aren't there, when you go out with a boat person? The prospect of the Gaumont on a Friday isn't going to be so attractive to someone who's had to row for their very survival.'

'I'm not sure they do row.'

'You know what I mean.' With a sigh he stood, brushed down his trousers, and wandered round the bench in tight, reflective circles, sweeping the air with his right arm as if being polite to an idea. Now and again Jim adjusted himself to follow this perambulation but, finding it tiresome in the long run, made an arrangement with himself whereby he'd only glance up as Jeff passed immediately in front. 'No. I hadn't been serious with a woman till Mei Lee came along. She's so different from any other person I've been out with. She's beautiful, for one thing. Scares me to death. I'll own up to that. Do you know, Jim – and I don't want to appear rude – but the women I've been close to so far have all had flabby arms. I don't understand it because flabby arms are one thing I can't stand. Personally, I can't. Flabby arms and a basket in the corner of the living room full of romper suits from jumble sales. Jacobson calls it the 'Bing Bong Wah Wah' condition – church bells, babies crying. I saw it as a joke too, till Mei Lee, and now it's not such a bad idea. Settling down. Stories at bedtime. My own lawnmower. That kind of thing. Do you understand?'

Jim understood and nodded in affirmation as his friend moved into the home straight, an ill wind catching the rumples in his shirt.

'Don't get into a state, Jeff. No one deserves to take out Mei Lee more than you, and if you don't mind me saying so, Mei Lee couldn't deserve anyone more suitable to ask her out. Be *Jeff*, that's the answer. Find a Jeff-shaped hole and slide into it. Don't worry about shapes which don't suit you . . . Though I would suggest you make a slight adjustment in your choice of shirt colour.'

'Oriental Sunset?'

'Well, let's call it pink for the sake of argument. I always think that particular shade, when coupled with a knitted tie, says things about you that aren't really true. In the immediate absence of a text, people always examine the cover first. And whether we agree with it or not, they make value judgements based on its design. Go *cool*, Jeff. Go cool. And the fawn trousers. I know you're doing your best but they don't carry the weight they used to. Perhaps you should aim for something more casual. I'm only guessing, but if you've been cooped up in a junk for weeks on end in search of freedom the last thing you want on dry land is to get tangled up with a guy in fawn trousers.'

Having reached the end of a circuit, Jeff dropped to the bench, placed his hands against his cheeks and squeezed.

'Sorry, Jim, but I'm going to stand up for myself a bit here. I'm with you to a degree on this colour of shirt – it was the only clean one I had left. But I'd argue about the trousers. At least she'll know she's dealing with a reasonable person. Not a football hooligan or anything. You don't see many vandals in fawn.'

Jim breathed in heavily. Something in the wind-sculpture of Jeff's hair reminded him of an Old English Sheepdog. He was suppressing an instinctive need to apologise.

'Anyway,' said Jeff, 'I don't want to go on about it. Jacobson only let me out for half an hour to catch a dentist's appointment I made up. He told me to make it back for the team meeting.'

'What the devil's a "team meeting"?'

'Oh, it's some new procedure he's cooked up. All about office democracy. In the meeting we're allowed to say what we think without him making a fuss. You'd have loved the one we had yesterday. Joe called him a tinpot Hitler, just to test out the democracy thing. I could see old Jacobson going purple underneath.' Laughing, he punched Jim on the shoulder. Finding no response other than a slight movement to the right, he took to pursing his lips as if in consideration of what to say next. Eventually he yawned and jigged his knees. 'I suppose Miriam will be here later.'

'She said she would be.'

'I quite envy you. Having a wife. At least you know someone out there's loving you. And that can be the most important thing of all these days.' He flexed his knee and scanned the sky for some time as if to prevent the yawn which ultimately broke around his mouth. 'Look. It'll be evening classes tomorrow, but how would it be if I came over again on Thursday night? We'd have more time to chat.'

'Yes, that would be fine.'

'Sorry if I was a bit niggly just now. About the trousers.' He raised his leg and stared at it, twisting his ankle from side to side. 'Suppose you're right in a way. I just haven't caught up, that's all. In my heart of hearts I've always wanted fashion to be unimportant, but maybe that's a bit naive.'

Jim touched Jeff's shoulder. 'No. You stick with fawn if that's what you want to do.'

Jeff clicked his tongue. 'God, I nearly forgot.' He pulled an envelope from his inside pocket and put it in Jim's lap. 'Sorry we've taken so long to get round to it. I meant to bring it last time I came.'

'Thanks.'

As he stood, a gust of wind raised a tuft of his hair which then refused to subside. He took Jim by the hand, shook it for much longer than necessary, took a step back and sighed, the pair of white fists tucked into his waist. 'Maybe I should buy her some Quality Street on the way back.'

'Go on. Bugger off.'

Laughing, Jeff walked away, making a slight adjustment in direction to accommodate the route of the acrobatic psychiatric patient, who had moved on to cartwheels. At the door to the hospital building he saluted. Jim opened the envelope to find a card with a print of a duck by Dürer on the outside. The inside had been signed by everyone in the office and by Mei Lee herself. Jacobson's greeting began, *May I, on behalf of the Town Housing Department.*

Miranda has just glanced out of the window over there to check I haven't committed suicide. I've never understood those who kill themselves to avoid death, unless choice of dark destiny is preferable to imposition. Remember, Miriam, those mixed messages from the vicar up the road: death a fine thing to the repentant, a beautiful place occupied by people like the vicar himself, all cream teas, jumble sales, sponsored custard-slice delivery to the town's old folk. Once a week he'd plop printed gospels through our door with a hand-written message underneath announcing the date of the next Hoop-La, if the weather was fine, or else fun and games in the hall to draw youngsters away from adhesive-sniffing and yelling four-letter words at policemen who are only doing their job at the end of the day and won't bop someone on the nose unless they absolutely refuse to be white. And once a month the vicar's non-alcoholic discos featuring Matt Monroe and the Ronettes where, by all accounts, girls in pleats danced till half-past nine with prayer breaks before and after – prayers similar to those at school, suffering little children to come unto J. You were soon writing letters to the vicar saying that, like everything else, the church was all to do with men and that if Jesus had been worth his salt he'd have had a few female disciples. Then, Miriam, becoming enamoured of the mood such letter-writing brought, you ventured onto the subject of hell, the place the vicar insinuated folk went if they turned down Matt and wore leather jeans. You were forthright in your condemnation of men who had come up with a vision of a God so shallow as to want repentance for following the natural inclinations we'd been given at birth; and to wheedle their way out of this thorny paradox, the vicar and others like him had dreamed up the tale of Adam and Eve, wherein earthlings had taken the issue out of God's hands and become sinful from the start. The moment a child's head popped out, its goose was already cooked – unless it went on to do something fairly radical, and fairly boring too, so you claimed. And was this view in some ways a defence of our ropes, Miriam? Our whips, peacock feathers, battery-operated games, your wrists and ankles tied with silk? And this only a couple of days after your first visit to the office to make a claim for benefit and yours truly breaking rules to become involved with what Jacobson calls 'clients' to mask his true opinion that they are dispensible humans scrounging off the government.

I remember you that warm afternoon, dressed in black, all moisture then, my brain wet with sentences for you, your damp hips raised, skins rumoured with sunshine between soft conversations in black crumpled sheets, room moving from light to semi-shade to darkness then back to light, unenthusiastic breaks for snacks, coffee, a shower in the bathroom with the frosted glass, weakening one another with creams, carrying you proud back to the black bed, staining pillows with our melting, smells of you ruining my blood, then perhaps we danced, this thing pressed against your white belly, a skintight smooch over an Indian rug to exposed floorboards by the window and back again, a hint of you on black wallpaper, then falling through you again, both of us so damp we couldn't hold on.

viii

We are all susceptible. The phrase kept repeating itself as he left the garden, testing his body by going the other way along the corridor, through Radiotherapy, and down another two flights of stairs, making light of the condition of his legs, the constant acidic indigestion and a general lightheadedness. He reached the subterranean corridor with its dark green carpet and whining fluorescent tubes. *All of us susceptible.* A few yards along he found an unlocked cupboard and sought sanctuary there on an upturned bucket with a cigarette, an edge to the silence, as if someone were with him doing much the same. Though the sides of the cupboard pressed against his back and feet, there was no rear wall that he could see, its absence receding with mops, racks of plastic bottles, tubes of sink cleanser, then a darkness untouched by the flame of his cigarette lighter. The world all fucking going out of shape like a fallen apple left in wet sun. His guts hurt. He dreamed of Laura to cheer his guts up – blossoms of scrubbing powder, wreathes of dust, his knees drawn tight. The cunning of imagination was able to present her eyes from nothing, though most chronic patients realise there are eyes, and then there are yet more eyes, come to fasten you with fairy tales. He could have spent weeks brushing the hair on her leg, the tickle of each one in his lips. Though there's always something unseen and unaccountable hanging against us like cobwebs from rafters, we frequently deny it. Tangled in his hair, the knowledge of her. Once they met in the scrapyard part of town, where roads were narrow, sticky with a mix of oil and dust and roamed by beer-bellied men. Her car steamed up as they talked through the problem of being reluctant lovers, not that they ever got round to it, but they figured thinking it was much the same, the way it made their abdomens flame. Watching another pair of steamers parked up ahead turned them judgemental: bastards *they* were. Off with their heads, and the bellied men came back and forth with rig spanners. Up on an oily bank a band of alsatians tethered to a burnt tree by black chains rattled as they snapped at customers coming for a nut here, a linkage there, while old men in trilbys limped by on their way from squashed, dark, brick council flats to the squat, dark brown pub at the corner where men hung out with black blondes, shotguns, cocaine. She wore a skirt of parrot green, her thighs Castrol soft as she wound her seat back by degrees though they did nothing because they'd become tangled up in words, so much so he could hardly say her name. Sunlight reflected off ranks of squashed cars. She was singing, *Hit me with your rhythm stick, hit me, hit me.* An old favourite of theirs. Ian Dury. A kind of bugger saint, his satanic mouth tight against the microphone. Now an opportunity for soliloquy, wondering why it is that every *sane* guy having read her words wanted to sleep with Edna O'Brien. Is it that rapture of sentencing, or those Western Ireland eyes? Laura had no idea, not being that way inclined as lorries squashed beside us to collect cubes of metal, businessmen's fleet cars in two-foot blocks, a part of us wondering if there were still businessmen inside one or two, club ties, monogrammed top-pockets and intercontinental socks among crushed wheel arches and fractured gear sticks. *Your dad's been unavoidably delayed.* That must be it. Western Ireland eyes and the sense of her having come from a more exquisite planet than the rest of us, so luxurious to touch she might melt if left out in the warm and flames of hair may thaw my soul.

Jim dropped his cigarette to the floor and erased it with his heel. Having brushed his shoulders, he crept out of the cupboard with a mop in his hand, but put it back when he saw there was no one around. His hand against the wall, he followed the corridor which ran in a semi-circle, bypassing Casualty before widening on the left to make room for the tea bar – the only place in the hospital where visitors could smoke without being castigated. They were separated from non-smokers by a white latticed plastic screen. Despite this he knew it was Christopher talking there with Miriam, the bugger with his filter tip nodding in zoological mode. Jim walked as swiftly as he could to the lifts, remembering already how her rust-coloured arms, freckles and all, had been lying across the white table towards him, Christopher that is, the zoo person who was an absolute wanker, though Jim still thought fondly of Miriam. After all, there was nothing more natural than making sure you had a second trapeze to hold before letting go of the first, no sense falling *thump* to the circus ring to ooohs from the crowd. If only Christopher weren't so beefy, with such a bulldog face and forearms thick and meaty as Popeye's (though lacking anchors). No fun thinking of your nearest being pummelled by such a structure, even if by all accounts he was St Francis himself with four-legged creatures, posing for the local paper with a lion in his arms, feeding the damn bastard bitch with a baby's bottle at Christmas time and giving rise to the headline SANTA CLAWS! And here the brainless bicep bugger was, sharing tea with an incipient widow.

Ting! The lift-door opened. A sweat had broken over Jim's forehead. He was joined on the next floor by some nutcase with an oxygen bottle who remained at the back of the lift when, having risen again, Jim was spewed out at his floor. He fought his way back to the side-ward, cleared a space for Jeff's card on the bedside cabinet, his belly, though not sick, twisting and sour, and the back of his throat foul with tiredness. He remembered a long-ago second invitation to Miriam's for tea, up the four flights to a room with views of the cement works, an environment – she joked – for hardened local men. They discussed the universe for half an hour, then spent the rest of the weekend in bed, Jim's habit of verse and celibacy all over her bedroom floor. Jokes in darkness of a wet Miriam at his side, her hand brushing wastelands of him, tracing the malnourished guts, his marathon-runner's arms. Half of him wanted to get up and go home, the other half was sinking into the mattress – that half-scream of souls for the cool delight of remaining lonely. It seemed as if his old life style hadn't existed for decades, as on the Monday morning he woke to songs from cockerels on the city farm and Miriam humming at her dressing-table, brushing on eye make-up, wearing nothing but a flash of triumph. Whereas he'd previously been a visitor to this country, its ways were suddenly native to him and he found himself fluent in both language and currency. Finishing her make-up she moved as he imagined a peacock might across the room and out of the door. She came back with breakfast. He rang in sick to work. How was he then, if not a thin, muzzly, unopinionated bloke of white shirts and lullabys just round the corner? A husky, sour-breathed untousled-haired daydreamer at odds with a world doing loop-the-loops, yet in love with its postcards of sinuous seas, pink and yellow headlands, the chirrups of wrens on telegraph wires, the complaints of old men raising hats on loveless Thursdays . . . And the dream he'd had – though bright – remained unkissed . . . Pavements overdosed and wet, all similar, plump-bummed girls coming by on bikes, boy-fondlers queueing at the public toilets, a long, gossiping road close to his flat, globular and green with tight cabbages; and the evenings at home, plaintive hours of Jacqueline du Pré, self-referential games of snap, breath against black window panes, sheets of paper staying poemless but becoming poems of snow in themselves, his shoes up on a stool, imaginations of Edna and Dublin (though he'd never been and would never go), those Grafton Street girls coming honey-haired to read novellas of their lives and thumb through his. Then a tapping of knuckles in the night on the other side of the road and in the light of a door being opened by a half-sleeping guy, he once saw a fruit-woman wearing blue dungarees. She talked to the guy for a moment, and then was let in. There had been something beautiful in her streetlight hair, her armful of what may have been pomegranates. And then a shadow of them both in the room upstairs.

ix

I was a reasonable pupil, though unable to keep my mind on the subject in hand. If you ever get to examine my school reports, you'll see those very words: *the subject in hand*. Oswald slouched beside me at our double desk, humming through his nose the latest by Billy J. Kramer and the Dakotas, a copy of which he'd slipped into Laurinda Hallpike's bag at lunchtime figuring she might put two and two together. How could he have known that – having got the sum right – she would gather with friends in the yard to discuss, not his musical tastes or generosity, but his Milky Bar thighs and unsightly proboscis?

   The teacher in this higher class reminded me of a tortoise, the way his head slithered from the neck of a white shirt to teach us the meaning of the word 'propaganda', which Oswald had previously joked was the term for a polite goose. How do you fare in your priesthood, Oswald, pulling sinners' lips to goblets of wine in hazes of incense amidst a chime of handbells rung by youngsters in the uniform of penguins? Each of us has one life and luckily we don't all want someone else's or what a farce it would be. Like this: a farce. Down with the trousers and race round a stage at the Whitehall. Oswald had an Alice neck, hands that do dishes, and a desk in which the books were carefully arranged. Mine was in such a state it took some effort to extract *Elementary Biology* with its sketches of children in their various stages of development. We loved best the one of the girl, her breasts appearing like miracles, boys' mouths beginning to ache for them simultaneously – and wasn't that a circumstance well thought out by our Creator? Only once in a blue moon did Oswald laugh at jokes to do with God, fearing he'd be pulled up short at a later date by some iridescent version of our form teacher, a suit of armour and no sense of fun. His rebellion had its limitations, and I've heard that in terms of living he's reached a kind of end too close to his beginning – which reminds me of something T.S. Eliot wrote, though I can't think what it is. Eliot came up with poems which we were taught to tease our way through as if inspecting a long-haired dog for fleas, fingers grooming through deeps of fur. *Aha*, we'd say, *here we have a symbol of something-or-other*. Why he didn't just come out with it heaven only knows – this being a curious aspect of poetry altogether, which no one adequately explained. Oswald and I shared the same double desk for ages, the teachers and subjects moving round rather than the pupils, so each flake of old paint from the ceiling, each nick in the desktop, each whorl of grain in the wooden floor became second nature, familiar in dreams, pursuing us as a location through our compositions, parts of speech, life-cycles of mayflies, the Nile Delta, pounds into kilograms, the Israelites – the rods, poles and perches of those last imperialist days when we'd recite parrot-fashion units of measurement going back to Robin Hood, and then not use them except in witticisms. *My bike's parked a couple of perches down the road.* Beside me, Oswald was smelling of flannels and Scots Porridge Oats. His life-cycle – unlike the mayfly – was governed by his nose, and I've always suspected that had it not been for that Roman object he would have become intimate with all manner of girls in our class, though whether he ever realised in the dark part of his bed that this more-than-generous feature was holding him back, who knows? He may have snuggled there quietly reducing it with low-grade sandpaper, as I tried with my nicotine stains, rubbing fingers till they bled. Somehow the stains remained. Meantime, Laurinda's thighs thickened, became fuller, softer, an amber shadow delineating lines of muscle and fat. Each movement of her legs (lapped up through an untidy row of desks which had conspired to give us a good view) caused Oswald to poke my ribs and point to those brown glories and their shores of navy blue, a heaven from which others were excluded. Though our heads would still recite verses from *The Owl and the Pussycat,* beneath the desk stirred an introduction to our downfalls. Mr Hook – the tortoise teacher – lighting up his pipe in class, whacking boys with a stick, girls on the bums with his bare hand, if he was driven to it, which he frequently was. And the glee in his eyes as pleated skirts slipped over thighs the colour of condensed milk. I may as well admit I deplored Oswald for pretending not to know anything but usually getting ten out of ten. A ten-out-of-ten boy with a four-out-of-ten life and E minus nose but with priestly qualities. Not J.B. of *The Good Companions*, which is spelt differently anyway, but servant-of-God priestly.

Laurinda never did come along the track that day at eleven, leaving us to scuff through fields, swishing hazel staves, till we reached the pool, undressed and broke reflections of ourselves. He'd been circumcised, though how or why he didn't know and his was a belisha beacon – a brief soft one which, had he been more fortunate, might have featured in one of those Dali paintings of soft things: *Landscape With Melted Penis*. Already his God was decreeing it should not be used for at least one of the purposes for which it had been intended. The world went on forever. We could walk all day and find no end to it. In the distance, on the crest of the hill, stood Laurinda's farm, and we'd sloop ourselves naked from the pool to lie like whitebait on our famous rock, wondering if she'd ever come. On and on, a waterfall at the far end, a busy stream leading from it to a dark copse of mossed limestone, full of vines the jackdaws clung to. Here roamed Bumper Daniels at weekends, his zip open in search of girlies, while Oswald and I were making wet footprint pictures at the poolside of octopuses imagined in the deeps, crevices moist with emerald fern, a world of skin and hair, goose-bumps, thoughts cooked up to make his beacon shine.

Jim folded down the corner of the page because he'd been admiring Laura's syllables again, like flames in his chest. At length these would be extinguished by facts causing him to sulk backwards yawning, telling himself off for anything the least bit sad since sadness is rarely beautiful when one describes it of oneself; so whereas 'Jim is sad' would sound just the ticket, 'I am sad' would probably make lookers-on beat their brows or their blankets and gather sleep. The weight of her hand was ever like being hooked on to living. A woman of courage with yesterday eyes. That old gearstick between us as scrapmen sang hymns and sunshine sank into the adhesive black road. Through the half-opened window on her side came smells of yeast and hops from the old brewery, the blue of her eyes like sky above a blue sea, one cigarette after another stubbed into her sliding ashtray, not Dvořák on the radio this time but songs interrupted on the hour by synopses of the news. We'd be relieved to hear the world wasn't ending, and to celebrate the DJ would play one of those modern synthetic tunes with a computer-generated melody interspersed, perhaps, by odd snatches of a living voice. Jim was temporarily feeling old because, unlike Laura, he could remember lyrics by The Swinging Blue Jeans and Brenda Lee, and he could hear her giggling like the sparkling rill rumour had it once ran where the scrapyards now lay, rank upon rank of dead cars crawled over by vultures with tools, cranes sunk half-way up their caterpillar treads in oil-moistened mud. And she was fresh as a riviera sea-wind, pebble-skinned, hair shifting colour with the vagaries of light, smelling as she did that day of dandelion wine or tendrils of weed clinging to a wave-washed rock, blue suns flashing through pine forests, heavy-laden mornings of dew and spider; or Autumn afternoons, leaves across tracks like dead hands appealing to God, old blue-ridge cider songs coming from the squat pub and scrapmen digging each other's fat ribs in appreciation of her Innisfree mouth. This power in the face of debilitation, some of her to genius and beyond, the all-of-it wrapped up cunningly in her until scrapman leaned into the window-gap and asked if she'd make room for a large trailer, and from dreams of cream-soda summers all white socks and hair of spun gold she became a woman again, starting the engine and releasing the handbrake, Jim slinking down like a decayed toadstool to avoid being recognised. A deathcap, perhaps, one bite and you're dead. Make the bugger a nightcap of them mixed with laburnum seeds. Driving out of town, they'd passed churches, the ruins of country houses, egg-and-bacon cafés with greased-up windows, removal vans jagged in the car-park, and all afternoon her legs were squashed against the driver's seat like sky-pools a boy loves to dip his fingers in for love of moisture, reflection, remembered landscapes under dull rouge moons.

* * *

On the bed waiting for Miriam, Jim figured the room to establish how much shrinkage had taken place, though as usual this was hard because most items within a given space were shrinking proportionately: flowers in line with cabinet, cabinet with bed, bed with the room itself, though as far as he knew he'd stayed much the same. The room was gorgeous with the smell of lavender. Not real lavender, but the chemical substitute coming from a mushroom-shaped air-freshener on the windowsill. Floral fragrances all year round are just one of humanity's miracles. Would she own up to having been with Christopher in the tea bar?

He'd known no one so well as her, yet she was the least familiar. He'd seen her in all conditions save the ones she developed when he wasn't with her; had come to know the spasms of her madness, her face in moonlight and its homicidal charms; the click of her shoes as she dusted, her reflection in the mirror when she was preparing to go out. He liked lying on her bed to spy as she moistened herself – the care she took, her naked back, her profile in the looking-glass, her open make-up bag, its rainbow squares, soft brushes. She would be silent and impervious to his questions. Together with her ritual evenings in the bath, making-up was a sacrosanct occasion. Pools of blusher on her cheekbones. Eye-shadow turning her wicked. Lip-coloured lipstick. The surgical application of mascara. As soon as she'd finished she'd rise naked from the chair to examine the shapes she made: her legs long, proportionate; her breasts rising with pride as she threw up her arms, arched her back, glanced at the mirror, then at him. Choosing knickers, pulling them up in harmony with a music only she could hear. The two or three yards between man and wife were a frontier. A rose-coloured brassière would cup her breasts, the snap of its straps on her sun-brown shoulders, that unfathomable valley of skin at her spine, a nakedness of underarms, her old-fashioned smells and secrets nestling in silken fabrics which shone and made whispers between her legs. Trying dresses, holding one against herself, then another, but usually returning to the first. This wasn't how he'd expected loving to turn out. Somewhere along the line it had slipped into a secondary phase over which he deliberated while looking through photo albums, watching television, or touching the waxed leaves of laurel trees. He'd come to know her; she him. Lying the dress over the back of her chair she'd choose a suspender belt and stockings for special evenings, rolled on to each foot in turn, pulled right to each fermented thigh where fingers, as they buttoned nylon to the suspender belt, made indentations in her soft skin. Like this she often decided to tidy round the bedroom, putting books back on the shelf, re-arranging ornaments or reaching over him to snuff the candle which had been burning on the chair, the inches of thigh at the tops of her stockings accidentally brushing his fist, an event for which he'd apologise, yet the coolness of her would linger there like old silken scarves. Then she'd move to the chair to put on her dress and shoes, glancing and smiling at him as, finally, she left the room. He'd be thinking this through. She was beautiful in a way finer than being beautiful in itself. The light of his experiences with her had added something, taken something else away. Now and then he hated her, though the hatred was inspired by a sense of disappointment rather than Miriam herself. This paradox of being familiar, and foreign too. And strangeness, though painful to the spirit and impenetrable to wisdom, is hard to substitute. The enemy of lovers who sometimes come by.

x

In here days are much the same, though his illness improves or deteriorates at the snap of a finger, lightening, darkening his attitude from dawn to dusk, while outside the weather most often fails to echo his mood. The bits and pieces of the town and the rooms within it continue to shrink, though too few care about it enough to converse openly on the subject. Shrinkage isn't news. If it was, a revolution might have taken place by now. But you know people – they hate it when things crack up, when routine changes (even for the better), or an old enemy suddenly wants to shake them by the hand. Peacemakers have more suspicious eyes. Jim smiles thinking of it now – his routine Monday. He'd woken at six-thirty as usual, made Miriam's coffee, given Buggerface a shout, wolfed a strong cup of coffee, then set about putting out the dustbin, washing his hair, listening to the radio headlines. Upstairs he heard Miriam singing. Not a usual thing. She la-la'd down the stairs in the folds of her favourite dressing-gown, threw an arm round his shoulder and slid her knee between his legs, but since his gut was up the creek he carefully unhooked her and put a couple of slices of bread under the grill. The postman brought news from her cousin Nathanial in Nova Scotia. Outside, a thick fog was making the town quiet as an attic at midnight. Jim dreamed at it through a window and burned his toast. Miriam glanced at him in a way which contracted his unskilled heart. As he tried spreading the cold butter, both pieces of toast snapped in half. Miriam was telling him cousin Nathanial had met a nice girl on a Nature Conservancy Weekend and was planning to marry her. They'd bought a cabin with a stream nearby, cool waterfalls and natural bears. *Give my regards to Jim.* Upstairs, Buggerface's attempted demolition of the ceiling was more persistent than ever, provoking Miriam to whisper 'piss off' as she covered her own unburnt pieces of toast in thin films of margarine and reduced-sugar jam. 'Cut the noise, you old croaker.' Maybe the unfinished thesis had been irritating him again. Life's like that. You're on the verge of finding an answer to it when, *splat!* Your dream of waking without hatred goes by the board. Miriam's knees a pink gateway now locked up for the moment. Jim crunched his way through breakfast, his thumbs covered in butter and crumbs of black toast – his mouth too, as Miriam later pointed out. Kissing her neck for old time's sake, he wiped his hands on the tea-towel and went to the bathroom to clean his teeth. She'd bought a new toothpaste which didn't guarantee anything at all. It was the latest thing. Neither did it taste of any form of mint. Jim noticed in the mirror a tendency for the flesh around his cheekbones and eye-sockets to contract. He'd become unrelated to a child he remembered and, like someone who's just failed a televised quiz, wished he could start all over again with the same questions. Life would have been much better had there been a teensy bit more information available. If British Rail could come up with route-maps and timetables, why couldn't God? A chap was just long enough alive to realise what mistakes he needn't have made. And the bathroom was indeed smaller. Lying in the tub the night before his feet had extended beyond the taps. As he wiped excess toothpaste froth from his lips with a damp towel, the phone rang and Miriam thudded into the living room to answer it. At first he thought it must have been Christopher making arrangements in code for a liaison before work, but when he came out of the bathroom Miriam was sitting on the sofa gazing at her knuckles.

Jim threw the towel to the floor. 'Who was that, this time of the morning?'

'Dr Matthews.'

'Couldn't he sleep or something?'

'He wants you to call round the surgery straight away.'

'Straight away?'

Jim had almost forgotten the blood sample he'd given a few days before. Miriam had persuaded him he ought to find out what was bringing him down. She reached up to hold his hand but he shook it off. He disliked sympathy in any form. She reminded him that he'd forgotten to comb his hair after washing it and it had now dried into something horrible. There wasn't time to sort it out. On the news, spacepersons had been reported landing in Yugoslavia. A woman called Olga was giving an eye-witness account through an interpreter. Disengaging the knot on her dressing-gown, Miriam opened her body against his Housing Benefit jumper and trousers. She was going through a phase. Like the moon. And like the moon her phases waxed and waned, though she had yet to let a man walk all over her. He could smell Christopher more than usual, those old baboon juices, the spit of armadillos. He wished to kill and love her. A game had been played for some time whereby he knew she knew he knew but she pretended he didn't, and on occasions their sex life had been given a new lease of life by the confusion. He kissed her goodbye, touching the globe of her backside through the soft cotton. She was making noises normally associated with a child unwrapping a strawberry split, and Buggerface's stick was now striking the ceiling in a slow, repetitive manner. As they kissed, a bird crashed against the windowpane. Miriam rushed into the garden but couldn't find it. She'd had occasion to blame such ornithological accidents on brain damage through acid rain. Jim knew better.

 The surgery was still in darkness and thick fog had pushed against its windows and crimson door. Eventually Dr Matthews came, leading him into a back room where the receptionist and cleaning lady were sitting in armchairs discussing neuralgia. Dr Matthews extended his hand towards the matching sofa, invited Jim to sit down, then rocked on his heels in front of an ornate china cabinet. Wasn't the weather awful? Patients had already been ringing in with fog-related complaints. How was Jim's wife? Jim tried to explain, but Dr Matthews wasn't listening. Rather, he was gazing at a piece of paper in his hand and wriggling his Scottish moustache. Whilst not wishing to cause alarm, it was his view the patient should be admitted to hospital that very morning. A gasp from the cleaning lady reminded Dr Matthews of her incongruous presence and led to her being noisily evicted from the room, her mop and bucket clattering against the doorframe. The receptionist was smiling like an infant teacher. No, Matthews wouldn't hear of Jim making his own arrangements to travel to hospital; suggested he go back home while an ambulance was summoned. For some time Matthews didn't speak and it wasn't till Jim managed to catch his attention and nod hopefully towards the door that the doctor waggled his hand and allowed him to leave.

Perhaps the ambulance had misinterpreted Matthews' message. Jim had hardly finished packing when it swung into the crescent, its blue light illuminating the fog. Blue was Miriam's favourite emergency colour. No siren. Jim slinked back into the shadows. Miriam was embarrassed because of the neighbours, who'd be gripping the edges of their curtains and rationalising themselves as not snoops. The crescent was full of them – not snoops. Buggerface had been brought down and was in the background playing with the hem of his favourite day-patient jacket, in front of him an untouched bowl of grey porridge with a melted pool of butter at its centre. As the woman in blue came up the path, Jim kissed Miriam, gathered his bag, shrugged towards Buggerface, opened the door and allowed himself to be led away, his head bowed but ears pricked to the first of the ambulance woman's humorous stories. Climbing the two metal steps into the back of the ambulance, he turned to see Miriam waving from the doorway, her figure erased slightly by the mushroom-coloured fog. She had said she would follow him to the hospital once Buggerface had been collected, and she'd rung the zoo and Jim's office. As the ambulance moved off, he watched her receding, fading away.

When they reached the main road the male driver turned on his siren to warn the heavy traffic which had built up, the weather exacerbating the normal morning rush. Healthy motorists were only too pleased to pull over. Jim waved each time, though he wasn't sure they could see him through the darkened glass. Gradually he became aware that the ambulance woman was squeezing his hand.

'Don't worry about the noise,' she said, nodding towards the driver. 'He just wants to get off on time. We've been on the go all night.' Jim hugged her thumb in return. He had respect for anyone whose working night might entail the gathering up of decapitated motorcyclists and didn't want to stand in their way by complaining of claustrophobia or the driver's reckless attitude towards traffic lights. With yellow streets slipping against the window, Jim's insides were doing somersaults, as if confirmation of physical illness had given them permission to deteriorate. Outside, people in grey overcoats were stooping to work, cramming into grey bus shelters or pounding along on racing cycles, scarves tied round their mouths. He thought he saw Laura standing in a doorway, though familiarity with such hallucinations led him to dismiss the sighting yet again.

The journey took less than twenty minutes. He was led to Casualty, where he waited in cubicle for well over an hour while a series of medical persons not from Britain tried to establish his identity, refusing to base their opinions on any information he volunteered to give. He played with needles in a kidney dish, discovered the meaning of his dreams in an old *Hare and Hound*, and swaggered to the toilets – where an old man who hadn't bothered to close the door was in the process of shifting his insides from where they are normally found into the vitreous china toilet bowl. Back in Casualty several cigarettes later, Jim was mistaken by a houseman on the brink of slumber for an overnight drunk and was being shown where to sign the discharge form when the nurse, who turned out to be Miranda, showed up and led him to this ward, this room, asking him first of all to undress. At his request, she pulled a curtain round his bed and left the room. He'd never come to terms with the fact that patients were supposed to feel unabashed about flaunting physical secrets just because they weren't tip-top. He acknowledged the moment of undressing as an exchange of one life for another, and as such regarded it as a sombre occasion requiring solitude. Someone took blood. Minutes later someone else took more blood. It seemed that the first person hadn't taken enough. Jim commented that as far as he was concerned they could take the whole fucking gallon. He didn't normally swear. This caused the second person to dab the sticking plaster onto the crook of his arm with some violence before stalking away. Other than Miranda, the nurses seemed to have made a decision to behave towards Jim as if whatever was wrong with him had been conjured up simply to annoy them. He lay in the bed, the top sheet folded neatly across his middle, his hands resting together above it, his gaze fixed towards the window. A man outside in a wooden cradle was rubbing the pane with a wet cloth. Before lowering himself to the next floor, the man waved his plastic bucket in salutation.

Jim held one-sided conversations with an unlistening deity.

xi

Jim was half asleep when Miriam came in. The sound of the door made him jump. She was laughing.

'Why have you got your clothes on?'

He arranged the pillows against the head-bar, then pulled himself into a sitting position. She kissed the hollow of his cheek.

'Pyjamas make me insecure.'
'Doesn't Sister mind?'
'She hasn't said anything.'
'I can't imagine she'd be too happy about it. Still, it's up to you.'

Jim stretched himself and drew up his knees while Miriam unpacked a paper bag: chocolate, pears, new underwear with diagonal striping. Having arranged these gifts on the cabinet, she sat beside him, keeping the tip of her left shoes in contact with the floor.

'Tell me what you've been up to then.'
'Jeff popped in.'
'Oh yes.' She picked up the card. 'It was a nice idea for everyone to write a little message, wasn't it? Who's this with the funny signature?'
'Mei Lee. A boat-person Jeff's in love with.'

His hand had accidentally touched her leg through the thick blue coat and she was blushing in response. He suggested she take the coat off. She was smelling of Hyde Park in November, dry cold pathways covered in leaves; had coloured her hair a shade between red and brown and it was shining under the strip-lights. Having returned the card, her fingers twisted together as though she were cold. This was Miriam. She wasn't going to take her coat off. He moved his hand away from her leg.

'And how *are* you today?'
He coughed. 'Oh, you know. Fine.'
'Typical. You can't be fine or you wouldn't be here.'
'But there's nothing I want to go on about. Gut is a bit delicate.'

'Well, you don't eat. A nurse mentioned it just now. No breakfast. No lunch. You won't eat. There's probably nothing up with your stomach. You just won't eat properly.'

'I don't feel like it. Sometimes the idea of it's all right, but when it's there in front of me, my appetite vanishes.'

'You should try anyway. I expect the bad feeling would ease off if you had something for your acids to work on.'

'I'll see how it goes. I'm not doing much either, and you know how I get when I'm in that situation.'

She hadn't realised that on last night's visit her foot hadn't reached the floor. If he mentioned it she'd just make out she was sitting differently this time.

'And how's Uncle Fucking Tobias?'

'Oh, don't ask. He had the runs in the night. I couldn't get a wink. Still, he was solid again this morning before he left. I was in a right old state by then. He seemed to think there was something funny about it, as if he was getting his revenge.'

Jim had changed his mind. He pulled the hem of the blue coat to one side and rested his hand flat against her skirt, though it seemed necessary to keep it very still. Through the material he sensed a heaviness in her thigh, a breadth to it. Beneath the unbuttoned coat she was wearing a white blouse with a ruff collar which hid her neck, and perhaps the zoo-man's teeth marks.

'No improvement in the old sod then.'

'Can't you guess? I think he's making half of it up. There's never anything wrong at mealtimes or when there's something he wants to watch on the telly. I've been thinking of getting him a portable out of the catalogue. He can watch it upstairs then.'

His hand had an imagination of its own, wanting to follow that black skirt to the waist, then trickle up the ribcage to her neck and make her shrug with the tickle of it – annoy her. Soulmates they'd often been in the kissing of limbs. Coming to the bed in times past she'd unwrapped them without ceremony, lamplight illuminating her skin, turning whites and light browns a coarse gold, softening those goosebumps. It was something to wonder at, this sunset of her flesh, his hands inviting her to his side; then the weight of her, bones and all, the fact of skin as she lay and wriggled at full-stretch, snuggling up. They always knew from the kind of kiss they began with where an encounter would lead, the all-clear being sounded by an intrusion of her tongue into his mouth and journeys of her hand to a capture of what it already knew. He loved his body then: streamlined, made beautiful in artificial light till even he could have touched it. Then . . . His hand on her cheek, which was invariably cold; round to her shoulder; part-way down the indent of her back. His fingers had travelled that way so often that now, with his eyes closed, he could remember her surfaces. In those days they'd hear the click of the gate, stiffen at someone's knock, wait, breath held, for whoever-it-was to retreat. A double-glazing man maybe – chance of draughtless cavities whistling on down the road. A couple of people in a room somewhere enjoying the extremes guts hungered for. Yet underlying that was a companionship of spirit, the immediate future already written, knowing at which point her hand would touch him *so* and at which point he'd fall towards her, having kept a certain admission of spirit to one side, hoping to reinforce some myth of malehood. There was no sense pretending she always kissed him in the way or where he wanted her to. Nor she him. They weren't courageous enough with the subject, not like moderns lying side by side afterwards holding an inquest. Rather, they had gradually abandoned themselves to the familiar, leaving imagination aside. Now the roughs and tumbles of early days were practised for a moment only to be abandoned for a more traditional outcome: the contentment of anxieties being swallowed up, tastings of Christopher. Perhaps Miriam thought of her zooman, and Jim of someone else; or maybe they had requirements they wouldn't dare reveal. It made little difference to objective realities. So what if they lay like flatfish afterwards, worn out and vaguely disappointed? He wouldn't have minded her saying so, but invariably they reared away from any dissection of fundamentals, scared, perhaps, that requests for variance might lead to insincerity or something 'not natural'. He didn't always experience what he would have recognised as love. Not really. Always those snowbound corners. The bad weather came, didn't it? And whatever a man was, he wasn't enough of one – always preoccupied, somewhat indecisive. At least he thinks he was. You see how lyrical a guy at her leg can become? Torpedoed and fucking sunk. In those December days she must have watched Christopher throwing meat to pumas, twitched as that stink of masculinity reached her. From the damn pumas most probably, but she'd have enjoyed it anyhow. I don't like being addicted to something in you. God shows himself a mean, cheating sloth at times. Remember when you attacked me with the bread knife and I stormed out and drove all over town determined never to come home but did so because I ran out of fury and cigarettes? On the doorstep you were talking to a discontented perfume saleswoman, and within hours of almost succumbing to the blade we were sharing chips. There's something for the spacepersons of Yugoslavia to chew over when they've come to grips with the rules of cricket: loving the person killing you. Like loving a God sending rains to people in no need of rains. Your thighs would smell of thigh cream. You rubbed it in night and morning to stall degeneration in the places you guessed laxity would succeed tightness; dullness, gleam; infirmity, power. Your breasts too, anointed with breast cream to maintain self-assertion, angle of nipple. Face with face cream, hair with conditioner. Standing askew to apply the creams it would become evident that some different beauty had crept upon you while you weren't looking; that maturity had some solemnly fermented attraction all its own – not scant or classically pretty perhaps, but replete, succulent, skin plushed with a deepening of subcutaneous fat, a broadening of hip making longer and more dramatic the slope upwards to your waist. You could say youngsters are the minutes of living, but hours should pass in the company of richer, less readily exhausted forms. Thus spake those Yugoslavian spacepersons. My mood goes in carousel round this smell you have, creams, Christmases, Christopher, his pitchforks, wheelbarrows, fruits for parakeets. The sherbet dabs of toddlers weaving through his zoological gardens.

Stroking her old man's hair, Miriam slipped from the bed and limped up and down. Her right foot had fallen asleep. Jim was studying the swing of her skirt and the backs of her legs; and in a game he played sometimes he was trying to picture her as someone he didn't know. As a woman pure and simple.

'I'd quite like to make love,' he said.

She had come to a halt by the window and was staring out, her right foot on tiptoe like a horse resting. 'Don't be silly, Jim.'

He rubbed his nose. 'I don't think it is particularly silly.'

'I didn't mean it like that. It isn't silly. But we're not at home. Everything's a mess. And you always say things at the wrong time.'

It was only as he reached from the bed to touch her hand that he realised just how much smaller the room had become. He pulled her till she unstuck from the window and came to his side, then toppled her on to the bed and rolled her close. Wriggling down, he opened her coat and lay his head on her blouse. She stiffened.

'Next door wants to know if they can borrow the lawnmower.'

He looked up to check she wasn't smiling. 'What's it got to do with me?'

'You're always saying you don't like them.'

'I was joking. You know I was only joking.'

'Thought I'd better check with you first. His blade snapped.'

'They shouldn't be mowing the lawn. It's too wet.'

'That's their problem, isn't it.'

'Why are you asking me then? If you want to lend them the bloody lawnmower, then do it.'

He could feel through the blouse a quickening of her heart. 'OK. But don't shout at me.'

He pretended to laugh. 'Here we go. That wasn't a shout. I'm not shouting, all right? Every time I disagree with you you say I'm shouting.'

'Raising your voice then. I ask simple questions and you raise your voice. I know you're not feeling well, but I still don't think there's any –'

Jim rolled away from her. 'Yes, I am raising my voice *now*, but that's only because you're telling me I'm shouting when I'm not.'

Miriam returned to her former position. 'Right, Jim. Let's not talk about it. We'll just add lawn-mowers to the list of things we don't mention.'

He thumped the pillow and turned his back. 'Sorry, but I can't understand what we're arguing about now.'

'I'm not arguing. You might be. I'm just irritated at you getting into a state over nothing. You're always the same.'

'Who's in a state? I don't see myself as being in any kind of state.'

'Why have you turned your back on me then?'

'Well –' he took a deep breath – 'you probably haven't noticed but I've been trying to get close to you since you came through that door and for some reason you don't want to know. Why shouldn't I be annoyed about that?'

'You haven't mentioned being close. Just sex. And right now sex isn't something I'm concerned with. Anyway, you said you weren't annoyed.'

'No. No. I said I wasn't in a state. There's a difference between being in a state and being plain old annoyed. I *am* annoyed. And who mentioned sex? Certainly not me. I said I'd like to make love, but that was a general observation, not something I was expecting to do here, this minute. A hug or some-thing would have been nice, but I bet you're just scared someone's going to come through that door and catch you in some position other than vertical. God knows why.'

She moved back to the window and gripped the sill. 'No. It's nothing like that. I'm just a bit tense today. That's all.'

'That's all? You're always tense.'

'There you go. I'm not *always* tense at all. When you're in a corner you always start generalising. I think it's quite reasonable to be tense in these circumstances.'

'OK, I'm sorry. You're not always tense. But the last thing I want is for you to be tense now. You seem to be forgetting that the circumstances you're on about are happening to me. By the same token, I don't think there's anything odd about wanting to be close to you right now. Sometimes it's like you're trying to avoid having anything to do with me.'

Her sigh misted an oval of windowpane. 'That's unfair and you know it. You should realise how upset I am over all this.'

He could tell by a shivering in her neck and shoulders that she would cry if the subject of distress were pursued. The perfume of creams rubbed in to keep her skin moist slipped and sparkled while he breathed in the flame and frostbite of being in her company. And then came recollections of lying wet next to her, full up and nothing to compare the feeling with, not even fantasy. Jim remembered her coming through the bedroom door and letting her dressing-gown fall to the carpet. A sunlit afternoon. Both on holiday. Buggerface at the day centre. An hour fiddling in the garden, then bed. The swing of sun against curtains swinging in wind from the open window. There were miracle days, then days of resentment over inconsequentials, the yesterday stinks of licking and pinching but never a reference to them in walks through town looking in shop windows at things they couldn't afford, this same finger tapping the glass when it had so recently played wicked with her. *In which case, always keep the nails trimmed.* This is brilliant. To follow mushrooms of dream in a sterile room, Miriam at the window in vain for arguments to pursue, skies of pastel when in memory she's still wet, crimson to her abdomen, legs in welcome, and his mouth resting *thus*, wishing thigh farewell. Wet and faintly blue his fingers or fist kneading a moistened belly, his hair moistened in the fruits of her.

'I planted fifty bulbs in the border at the weekend.'
'You told me yesterday.'
'Did I?'
She folded her arms. Jim swivelled round with the intention of going to her but changed his mind. He'd been thinking of things to say but all of them sounded made up, without conviction or sincerity. So we tanned his hide when he died, Clyde, and that's it hanging on the shed. Shed was it? Or shack? He checked his watch, then lay back, guarding his eyes against the fluorescent tube.

'They'll look lovely in spring. I'm thinking of planting more cowslips too. Not from seed, that would take too long. I've found a shop which sells them pre-grown. They're more expensive but –'
'Yes. Do that. I like them.'
'Anyway.' She was watching the faint image of herself in the window and flicking its hair.
Jim put his hands behind his head. 'When are you coming in again?'
'You want me to go?'
'No, I didn't mean that. I just thought you were

about to go. You usually are when you sigh and say "anyway".'

'I didn't realise I had said anyway.'

'Yes. Just now. So? When are you coming in again?'

'Tomorrow some time I suppose.'

'You don't sound too enthusiastic.'

She turned round quickly as if she'd gathered herself together. Smiled. 'You'll have to stop this interpretation of me all the time. I don't like being too specific in case something comes up. I'll be here as early as possible. I won't be able to manage this evening because Mrs Jellings can't look after your Uncle. Bingo she said.'

'More J's.'

'What?'

'Nothing. Just something me and Jeff were talking about earlier.'

'So if there's anything you want me to bring you'd better think of it now.'

Jim was admiring the way her leg appeared at this particular angle, its skin catching yellow light and, beyond her, a soft of autumn drenching the sky blue and white. He could have kissed the dips at the backs of her knees, their blue whiteness an old friend. As she turned more towards him he saw the outline of her breast cupped in white cotton, held there, and there was no one so unknown or so untouchable as one known too deeply and for so long. He'd been rebellious about falling all his life, like a child at the confectioner's unwilling to make up his mind. Those slopes of white and light, the thousand times of fingers dabbling music on a ribcage he could tell was hers in blindfold. He dreamed best of all when he didn't like her. Smells of cream, pickling vinegar, macaroons . . . *don't say vinegar, say Sarsons.* The beast would relish a simple journey into raw crevices where philosophies drown and love might find one belly flat and cold against another, his breast flattening hers, the rhythm of moisture. Part of loving, it could be, this quiet dislike, the distress of needing more than oneself as if a god (chuckling) wanted it that way, the frisson (if that's the word) of hair beneath her ear so faint only a tongue could discover it. Speaking in them, tongues, speaking in the tongues of bedtime through jungles of loving, cutlass-severed stems, water cupped on broad, jade-coloured leaves, the exposure of caverns draped in vine and silent but for echoes of running water, those overhangs of scented undergrowth. Parting it wilfully, then slipping into the dark. Making it up as he goes along. Fucking jungles. Who wouldn't chuckle over that one? A man may only invent so much before he faces accusations of impotency. If he dreams too often he can't be a decent fucker, surely. The poet's erection is softened by too much rhyming, so the gossip goes: too many storybook girls and an incapacity with the overworld where everything makes sense and has structure. Beneath it lie languages of chaos.

'Well?'
'No. I can't think of anything.'
'You can always ring if you do.'
'You are going then.'
She sniffed. 'It's one of those days, isn't it? I think it might get worse if I hang around. Maybe tomorrow you'll be feeling better.'
'What do you mean, me? I thought you were the tense one.'
'There you are you see. That's what I mean. Look,

I'm not trying to blame you for anything but we're going to end up arguing, and that would be unbearable.'

'*I'm* not going to argue. There's nothing worth arguing about as far as I'm concerned.'

'Anyway.' Coming to the bedside she tried to kiss his cheek, but he moved to one side. 'I'll see you tomorrow then. Don't forget to ring if you want anything.'

Jim reached for his cigarettes. 'And you have fun.'

'Should you be smoking in here?'

Lighting one, he lay back and blew inexpert smoke rings. 'No one's said anything.'

'And you wouldn't take any notice if they did.'

'I don't see the point, really.'

'Still, it's not as if you were in with the others.'

'Something like that.'

Though she had the usual familiarities about her, there was a subtle change of posture, evoking dim recognitions far within which frightened him. Something *else* in the movement of the backs of her legs, some echo in her voice – of a nightmare perhaps, or a fracture of reality. He pulled her down and kissed her mouth. This time the avoidance was hers. Her lips slid away from him. She was laughing. 'It worries me when you come at it like that.'

'You keep kissing my cheek.'

'Well, it was obvious when I came in you didn't want to be kissed anywhere else, that's why.' She stood up, buttoned her coat and took a step backwards.

'How was it obvious? What are you talking about?'

'Don't pretend, Jim. Anything else, but don't pretend.'

'You've cracked. At last you've absolutely cracked.'

'Don't start that. I'm not going to be pulled into one of those rows where I end up thinking I don't know what I'm talking about. You're an expert at that.'

'For fuck's sake, Miriam. I haven't a clue what you're saying.'

'OK. Leave it for now. I think I'd better go home. I'm sorry things have gone astray. Let's be sensible and leave it till tomorrow.'

She moved to the door with the walk of someone window-shopping, restricting the usual tom-cat thump out of reverence for his condition maybe. He'd been hoping to call her back before the door closed but somehow the words wouldn't come. When she was out of sight he took hold of the pillow, pulled at it as if trying to rip it open, then threw it at the cabinet, knocking pears, the bar of chocolate and *The Blue Kiosk* to the floor. A cold sweat was trickling from his underarms and for a few minutes he couldn't keep his breathing under control.

xii

Oswald had arranged for Laurinda to meet us by the oak tree in the glade at noon and now, as we followed the path through the wood, he was chuckling to himself.

'Tell you what. If she shows up, why don't you say you have to go to the dentist's or something?'

'Fine, Oswald. If she comes.'

'Oh, she'll come. I told her I'd have some Toffos with me.' He pushed his hand into his pocket and drew out the long tube. 'See? She loves them.' He nudged me in the ribs. 'And I've brought a tanner just in case.'

I was watching leaves, branches, green go by, a dozen different shades falling to the path. Time was slow and plentiful as lichen-covered roofs. Oswald had dressed up in the Catholic equivalent of drainpipes and a brushed velvet Beatles waistcoat his Mum had bought him for Christmas. He was going through a phase of wanting to be groovy. I could smell last night's rain, which had been so heavy and prolonged it had woken up the whole inn and by morning had made silver pools on the tops of the empty wooden barrels standing outside for the draymen who came each week in their thick grey aprons to collect empties and hang around for laughs over a pint or two.

'Ronnie reckons she's ready for it anyway. If he's right maybe I won't need the tanner.'

'How does he know?'

'I'm not sure. He just said he had a bit of news and that he'd tell me if I gave him threepence.'

Expensive fantasy. One of those dull, twelve-sided coins with a daisy on the back. Daisies or chives. We didn't care. Some threepences were worth a shilling if you took them to old Harris the dealer, and some shillings were worth five bob. I hoped to make a fortune one day, starting with threepence and working my way up. But my greatest dream was to come across one of those pennies withdrawn from circulation when old Edward the Eighth got tangled up with that woman. Oswald was smelling of genitalia. Crazy of him to leave Toffos in his pocket so close to the source. Toffos and threepence: the cost of Laurinda Hallpike was mounting. One of the more expensive girls we'd known. Yes, genitalia some mornings, incense on others, as if he'd been to Mass chanting Latin to the rhythm of sweet boys in surpluses who were beaten up by other boys (not Christians) in the youth club yard afterwards. Kids loving God or hockey or French knitting had consequences to endure, though maybe they were compensated by hardly ever having scabs on their knees or needing to wipe noses in month-old handkerchiefs.

Oswald was slightly ahead of me when a crackle made me turn. It was Laurinda rising from bushes, pointing at Oswald and shaking her head. I nodded to her. She was slinking back into the undergrowth with her scruples as Oswald sang 'I'm Alive'. Suddenly he stopped and was gazing into the pattern of leaves and sky.

'I think I'm always going to love her.'

'Straight up?'

'I can't sleep for thinking of her. It's just as if it was meant to be. When I'm alone I like putting on Mum's Nat King Cole records and going through all that's happened with her. She let me walk with her to the other side of the cricket pitch the other week before we broke up. When you were away with your tonsils. She didn't say much but she didn't have to. I'm thinking of buying her a copy of "Too Young" next. I don't 'spect you know what I mean about real love.'

'No.'

'But don't tell anybody, will you? There've been others I've liked, but she's the tops. Mum thinks I'm too young to be in love but what does she know, eh? Parents never know anything. Everyone has someone special eventually. Mine's come now.'

We reached the glade. Oswald checked his Ingersoll several times, shaking it, then climbing into the lower branches of the oak tree to scan the vicinity. He thought it would be a good idea if we sat either side of its large trunk to look in both directions. After half an hour he was still arguing with himself, inventing reasons for her lateness which started out as condemnations of her father but soon worked their way round to food poisoning and death.

'I hope you're still watching,' he called. 'Can you see anything?'

'Just trees and the path, Oswald. I don't think she's going to show up.'

'No, she will. She'll be here. She promised. We'll leave it a bit longer. There must be a good reason. Laurinda's not the sort of girl to leave me here like this. She told me wild horses wouldn't keep her away.'

Even the oak leaves were wishing in the wind. The famous tree was twenty feet round. It had a history of outlaws, kings in its branches, and executions at its roots. A long silence from Oswald came – as it later turned out – while he gouged his and Laurinda's initials into the bark with a penknife. They are still there now, widened and discoloured by the intervening years, a reminder of having waited right through dinner. Oswald broke his silence eventually by proclaiming he didn't care anyway, then throwing an old tin can at a squirrel, which hopped into another oak and flew among its branches. I was watching Laurinda laugh and tease from bushes on my side of the tree. She was putting her fingers in her mouth to pull faces or placing her hands on her cheeks and waggling her head from side to side. Between performances she ducked out of sight. Her games became more adventurous. Knowing already the structures of torment, she would lift her T-shirt till it almost reached the scraps of her breasts, then slowly sink behind the bush. I was building an abstract castle in the soil with the tip of an old stick. Each tease demanded a development. A little later she crept into full view, turned round and proved Ronnie wrong about the cost of seeing her without knickers by bending down, hoisting her skirt and rolling her hips from side to side. My first bum. Oswald was singing 'Norwegian Wood'. White bum with a slight shadow at the base of its divide which lost itself then in a whiteness of thighs, so pure I could have hallowed them; and as if to rub it in she had placed her hands either side of the divide and acted out a rhythmical dance to Oswald's untuned lyric. I managed a soil slope to the castle's courtyard and a shallow moat, glancing at Laurinda as much as propriety allowed, taking note as she threw caution to the wind, turned to face me again and pulled her T-shirt clean off, tossing it into the bushes from whence she'd come. There was something about girls which was best left alone. My insides thumped. She was pretending to be a cover-girl, raising her arms, linking her hands, pushing one foot forward and throwing out her chest. Her belly button a divinity of shadow. Sad but necessary he missed it. I was right all along that a breast in the imagination is worth two in the landscape. They were hardly there at all, and somehow didn't matter as such at the time as they would do the next night or the following year or in later decades. Those indistinct folds capped by pink moments. I formed the opinion it would have been better had she not known I could see her. Naturally her skirt followed, and it appeared her thighs were nestling nothing more than a cracked pink shadow. The white sniper, as we would later call it, preferred suspicion to fact and remained unmoved. The tip of my stick created a small well in the centre of the castle courtyard. She was naked, rubbing with her finger that shadowed crack, then spreading her legs and arms, a pale, beautiful X. After 'Norwegian Wood' we had a rendering of 'I Feel Fine', Laurinda caught by the faint greens of moving leaves, the blue of sky. Abandoning the X at last, she placed her hands at her ankles (such blissful stooping!) and drew them very slowly up her legs and thighs, over her hips and abdomen to her breasts, then threw out her arms once more to bow before darting back into the bush, and coming into view moments later dressed, but with a broad grin on her face – she curtsied.

'It's pointless waiting any longer. Let's go home,' I said as she slipped away again.

Oswald stopped singing and came round to my side of the tree, gazing miserably at the deserted wood. I stood up and stamped out my abstract castle. The heat of the day was intensifying. As we walked away he turned frequently to study the receding glade.

'I bet she's there now,' he said, his natural mucus intensifying too, getting the better of his nose. In that shroud of disappointment he was becoming the most unattractive boy in the region, now heavy with genitalia scent, Matins, warm southern Italy, shoulder-blades disrupting the line of his Beatles waistcoat. He was avoiding the truth of his being something of a toad dragged from a pond, his best qualities resting in his soul rather than in the arrangement of his ears, nose and multi-directional eyes, which ever gave the impression they were arguing among themselves over where to look next. Noses are one of the few things which are more beautiful the less you have, unlike gold. And the currency of nose held by Oswald had fallen into a state of aesthetic devaluation. The youngest children can be forgiven for them, but as time passed it was obvious Oswald was being seen as the instigator of his own nasal abundance and that therefore the blame should always lie squarely on him.

The history of guilt began a while later when Laurinda and I played in one of her father's barns. The game had developed into a mutual exploration of our lower quarters with hot fingers till Mr Hallpike's Friesian boom rocked the heavens and we scurried out the back way, adjusting our clothes as we ran towards the hawthorn bushes and hid there, giggling, out of breath, over-excited. Oswald, old friend, wherever you are, the afternoon had been nothing more than a happy accident, one of those rare times when the dreams of boys are achieved, bettered. When a close friend loves a girl it's only natural to half love her yourself. Her legs were smooth as still waters running deep and, as I'd already guessed, the hook of her was smooth too – the shadow there had been just a shadow of shadow itself. She laughed excessively as we made our examinations, so I suggest you wouldn't have liked her anyway. She would only have satirised your matrimonial intentions, thrown casual sarcasms at your nose during rows, been entirely unsuited to a person of your calibre. You needed then I believe, some Virgin Mary with added sauciness – the sauce essential so that when the time was right you could dally without loss of significance. You see, to Laurinda's way of thinking, the dalliance was all. Beyond it she cared for nothing. She was a surface with no substance – a fact proved by her exhilaration at being searched from the insides of her T-shirt and skirt. Pray for me, Oswald. I knew not what I did. Laurinda and the hawthorns of a hot farmyard beating energy from us, cows' tails raised in the pen close by. Believe me, she made it her aim to taunt some poor devil to death and the devil was me that afternoon, a Lucifer of unmetrical verses, stubborn genius, irrational fear. Nightmares of milk, gargantuan mouths, huge rubber balls. And you knew how fickle skin was in those early days, hungry for any scraps it could muster, and maybe it stays that way, though getting reinterpreted as an adoration of stars and the expression of that adoration with paper, words, adoration at one remove. Then again it might all be twaddle, Oswald, the quick mind convincing a guy each time of the validity of his illusion. Maybe you did the right thing, throwing it all away, turning your attention to a power which at least doesn't dominate your dreams. I can assure you, Oswald, that each suckle of the flesh erodes some finer but unclear ambition so that – in terms of sculpting for example – each coupling puts paid to another Venus de Milo. The more you give in, the less worthy any work becomes, so my advice is to keep walking with the Lord and find, among those grumblings of unspent flesh, a haven of creativity. It's that or some tickertape of unsuitable and short-lived wonders.

xiii

Nonsense. *The Blue Kiosk* was full of it, reflecting the charmed neuroses of an uptight world. Jim was at the window thinking it through as Doris came in with the afternoon drinks. Having poured his tea she carried it to the cabinet as usual, but this time the swathe of her overalls had difficulty negotiating the narrowing gap between the bottom of the bed and the wall. She smelt of bleach and damp living rooms. A pair of extraordinarily thick ankles were swinging from her frayed hems, and it wasn't easy to miss the ears tucked like crimson rocks in a rough white sea.

''Ere we are then.'

'Thank you.'

She wiped a stain from the cabinet with the hem of her overalls and took his old cup to the trolley. ''Ere, I gotta tell somebody. What d'you think? Caught young Doctor 'oosit in the store cupboard with a nurse 's'mornin. 'E was standin' there with 'is arms wavin' like this – and she was bawlin' 'er eyes out. Corse, the doc told me to get out, as if I didn'ave no right to be there. I told 'im, Look, matey, you might be a doc but its me what uses the store cupboard. We keep our Vim and wot 'ave you in there and its about the only place we can 'ave a fag. So anyway, the nurse runs out in a state and 'e looks me in the eye with a glare – like this – and slams the door. I thought, bloomin' cheek! I spect 'e's been 'avin a bit on the side with 'er and now 'e's fed up. Wants shot of it. 'Appens all the time in 'ere. That's why junior doctors are always on the telly moanin' about 'ow tired they are. It's nurses, not long hours. If they kept their 'ands on their stethoscopes instead of their you know wots there'd be no problem. Oh they'm buggers sometimes. Still, I don't s'pose you can throw 'uman bein's together in the cauldron of sufferin' and not expect plenty of 'ow's yer father. Bit like the war in that respect. We were at it like rabbits in them days. You always 'ad it in the back of yer mind this could be yer last. Dare say *you'd* be on the job if you weren't so knackered, no offence mind. No, it wasn't so much wot they were doin' but that they 'ad to do it in my cupboard. I mean, fair's fair. Tell you wot, give me back thirty years and I'd be in the bloody cupboard, too right I would be. Still, there's a lot to be said for gettin' past it. My George might not be Burt Lancaster any more but 'e comes 'ome on time and don't 'ave no bad 'abits. Not *them* sort of 'abits any'ow. Give 'im a pigeon and ten Woodies and 'e's appy as Larry. Gawd, look at the time and 'ere's me gassin' away. I'll 'ave that ruddy Sister after me.'

Jim stirred his tea. It was immensely pale brown with atolls of scum over its surface. Though it sickened his guts, he sipped it till Doris hauled herself away, calling her warmest 'Toodaloo!' A pale blue cup with matching saucer. Two more biscuits. He'd been thinking of Laura and her mouth on his like fragrant marshmallows, dreaming of eiderdowns, her arms in the night, those sleeping unrealities to sweeten nightmares, her hair and shoulders comfy to this lord of imagination, though she knew too well illusions were just enemies in disguise. Killers. She mentioned it. Parked this time in a side lane behind the abbatoir listening to cattle having bolts through the brain in the name of cellophane pies – so much so she felt sick and they had to move onto the black riverbank. It was all black, wasn't it? Even the greenery. All black. The excrement of people and passing traffic. Illusions were tipping him towards a darkness, but a darkness sweeter for being dark . . . So they discussed Hamlet, who had to be drawn to bitterly cold battlements before coming up with his finest words. Beauty is often sorrow in a change of clothes. Her eyes the blue of . . . well, cornflowers. She pulled away from him, laughing, and his secret was growing beyond its confines, an ugly secret with chicken skin and a tight, iridescent shaft, but much-of-a-muchness anyhow, nothing there to distinguish it from a billion others. Probably a billion. She had wound the window down and was looking out – grey daylight getting caught in her hair – at a line of trapped traffic stretched there on the wet main road at the far side of the river. He was thinking she was a beautiful person, no less, like a movement of sea over rock or the dazzle of sun from sand at low tide. Further along the riverbank stood a row of decaying wooden sheds and a half-submerged yellow bus, above it a line of pale homes with subsiding back gardens, green pigeon lofts, rusting clothes-line poles, wet kitchen windows misting up with living and dinner. Something classical played on the stereo because she loved incidental music to these unresolved typescripts and was describing a wooden house the composer built on a lake and the dependency she'd developed on his Fifth Symphony. Jim looked round in time to see Buggerface coming by in his day-centre minibus – one of his weekend outings, most probably – and while she laughed Jim was praying the old sod's condition wouldn't improve sufficiently to tip him into clarity and the relating of surprises to Miriam. Laura by this time was playing charades and he was supposed to unravel the symbol of her bouncing on the handbrake, fondling the button at the top. A man hummed past them in an electronic wheelchair, giving them a honk from an old fashioned brass horn attached to its side. Seagulls like fat Irishmen laughed at their own jokes. Behind the wheelchair man enormous red-bricked warehouses with barred windows loomed and fifty yards further on slabs of cold marble waited to be inscribed in the ramshackle yard of a monumental mason. The yard had a low fence but no barbed wire because no one, she supposed, would bother coming along to steal embryonic tombstones in the night. He was saying, 'Haven't you noticed how the town is kind of squashing up, becoming cramped?' And went on to relate how its atmosphere was bringing him down, as if he was trapped in an underground train stopped in a tunnel; and how old shoppers were having to squeeze past one another with baskets of apples while above them in small windows the white faces of melancholy asexuals marked the passage of time. Refusing to involve herself at that point, and with a certain blue joy in her eye, she was moving in a way which made her cobweb shirt ride high, fall from warm-hair thighs opening to daylight, parting; and where the flesh met higher up came a kind of unkissing to a stroke of plump crimson containing her, dreams of throwing off responsibility, the cotton wet just there, soaking, so his guts swung for her and her countryside smile, loving the conjure of her wet belly, garments with the softness of fantasy itself. Still ignoring his question she was resting on the root of that handbrake, her palms flat against the windscreen, though it all turned out to be a joke or satire about his conversation. A time of looking at the landscape through car-windows, the charms of woman and girl about her, all wound up. Men in stiff trousers and metal-capped boots were tracking from betting shop to the river and back, searching out dog-ends or scraps of news, then clumping together on corners to compare information. 'Well,' she said at last, 'now you come to mention it . . .' Pleased as punch, he was, to have someone share this fundamental outlook and laugh over the way his hair touched the roof of her car. Such moments. Jim was storing them up, though they raced by at the time, fixing them with context, meaning. She mentioned the dread she had of being a normal bastard, whatever normal meant. She'd seen examples of it and hadn't been the least attracted. An abnormal day has more impact when you think it through, and when all is said and done the memory is all. She would slump from brilliance to quiet reflection, her cheeks rounded like hamsters, he thought, her skin clear and uninjured by incorrect diets or by time itself – which was exacting an exorbitant toll on him, turning him into a kind of adman's focus for over-the-counter remedies. Packets of this for his bellyache, a tin of that for a certain soreness of throat. Zubes. She laughed at them, repeating the name under her breath. All afternoon she referred back to them. Zubes. And when a woman mentions Zubes a great deal, her hesitant admirer can't help but attach the memory of her to tins he later sees in chemists; so though Zubes may relieve a certain raggedness of throat, the soul gets buggered up each time he pulls out the tin.

Wednesday

i

As far as he knew, he hadn't been seen. It was just after nine by the hospital clock as he crossed the yellow-striped ambulance bay, followed the concrete spiral staircase to street level and pinned himself against a pebble-dashed bollard to catch his breath. In the open air his weakness had immediately widened; yet he had no doubt that, taking it slowly, he might go further than he'd imagined. He loosened his grip on the plastic bag he'd brought, having read somewhere that such white knuckles were a bad sign. Maybe he didn't look too good, but that was true of many of those walking up and down the road – uptight, frightened-looking buggers most of them. From this level the town appeared to be shrinking more quickly than he'd noticed from his room. The side-streets themselves lay closer one to the other, and the main road, though still reasonably broad, had less substance than in the old days, kind of excusing its own journey through ranks of green and yellow buildings; beyond them the chemical-works chimney had compensated for a diminished width by reaching further into the sky.

Autumn was a songless speckled bird standing motionless on the guttering of the double-fronted ironmongers; and the town itself, as exemplified by pedestrians, hummed, whistled and passed the time of day, though now and again it came across an inconvenience of this shrinkage and complained under its breath. Time was a melodrama running on and on through queues of traffic, a haze of their collective exhausts. Old men in suede shoes. Young, black-hatted women carrying tambourines. Sunshine picking out the pink and maroon diagonals of a plywood harlequin leaning into the street from a bracket above the doorway of a gift-shop whose windows were full of brass and cut-glass gifts, souvenirs to remind the buyer of those glow and feather days, each gift with its own printed box. He would walk to the museum as an exercise. He wasn't too far away. As he began his attention was caught by a man and a woman walking towards him, their arms locked round one another. They were both elderly and out of shape. Each time either of them spoke, the other would laugh as if the day to them was one long, fond reminiscence, and it was clear neither of them could or would have seen Jim as he passed with the almost empty plastic bag dangling from his left hand. Here as well as anywhere he remembered Miriam hanging back every few yards to dream in front of shop windows, spending what she didn't have as a cheap sedative, whereafter she'd chew her finger at home in a ruin of non-purchase. He was passing the theatre whose boards were advertising a small-time comedian. A fruit-stall had been set up at the top of its white steps. Oh, what an indulgent pastime it is. The woman serving was again familiar in her blue dungarees. He'd have bought an orange but courage had fled. No point buying an orange from her because she'd ignore him and ruin his living. Blue dungarees, and a remarkable way of not looking at him. Still, why should she be interested in a patient on the run or, in this case, on the crawl. Miriam's smell long ago had been similar to his: the sap of having joined in sports of rope, stained sheets, pastoral wrestling – neither of them imagining more than they already had. They called it a *relationship* in the modern way, forgetting that even those who choose to ignore and stay away from one another through surfeits of loving are having a relationship. Everyone on earth is having a relationship with everyone else even if it is in terms of non-communication, fear, or plain indifference. Was this a remission? A flicker of latent energy? In any event he hated the term relationship, people screwing each other up prior to saying hello for the first time. He'd get angry in a minute, just see if he didn't. He glanced back at the fruit-woman. She wasn't watching after him, unless the truth was she'd had time to look away, having sensed he was about to do it. Glance at her, that is. Oh, if he had a pound for every . . . Given freedom, he'd recover and move to Venus. He'd had time to notice a badge she was wearing showing Tigger in yellow, and he was in quiet love with her before striking his leg against a waste-paper bin cemented into the pavement. Topped with polystyrene cartons. Thirty-second ratatouille. Was that Art Garfunkel singing 'Crying in My Sleep'? And where the fuck was he coming from? Where was Art coming from? Who was he to influence people's romantic attitude? Poetic misery selling millions. So *that's* where he was coming from – the pullover shop. A shop full of pullovers. The woman there behind the counter was wearing a pullover but not selling any pullovers because there were no customers. Everyone in the street seemed quite happy with the pullover they already had. A frightful week for the proprietors of pullover shops all over the world. Jim leaned against the bookshop window as if he were waiting for someone. Half-way to the museum. He nodded to those who looked at him as if to say: 'Yes, I'm waiting here outside the bookshop.' Then, having recovered, he walked on, the blue flagstones irregular under his feet, the walls beside him dirt-covered to a level of, say, two feet through years of splashing, like a tide-mark. Find ten things beginning with T starting from . . . *Now!* Tyres. Ties. Teapots in the window there. Timber. No, not timber. Timber's cheating. Toddlers. Tagliatelli. On the blackboard outside the restaurant, though that's cheating too because it's the word tagliatelli rather than the substance. Don't count tagliatelli then. Turret. (Miriam and I once had an Old Sumatran in that little place over there. She'd been suffering phantom neuralgia.) Thomas the Tank Engine (counts as one). Trousers. Of course, trousers. Always miss the obvious. Train. Truck. One to go. T. T. T. Troglodite? No. No Cabinet Ministers round here. Ticket. Well done. Ticket on the pavement. Just there. Only those with the keenest vision could have seen it. Rooster Bus Company Ltd. 45 pence. And what's that in red? Oh, for Christ's sake: *Have a nice day.*

He pulled himself up the steps and pushed through the revolving door into the spacious main hall of the museum, which was lined with the same paintings, sloping show-cases and suits of armour, though the side-bays had been used to house a new display called *Man Through the Ages.* In the first a pair of primitive papier mâché peoples (Jim wished he'd been doing P) were crouched next to a fire made of coloured cellophane. Behind them was the mocked-up entrance to their cave. In another bay stood a sarcophagus whose painted front would swing open to reveal a mummy if you placed twenty-pence in a slot. Elsewhere were knights. Romans, Tudors with big bums, young women in Victorian parlours doing needlework and, towards the end of the hall, next to a marble staircase, a wax man and woman holding portable telephones to symbolise how far we'd come. At the top of the stairs, in 'Miscellaneous', he came across the broad antlers of an elk-like creature which had once roamed Basingstoke, the shields of Maori warriors, a case full of Roman coins, a man in blue wearing a cap standing in a corner with a handful of information leaflets (one of which Jim refused), a William and Mary dining table, a tableau of Florence Nightingale attending to a patient whose nose had obviously been re-glued at some point, various landscapes of this area long ago, before the Irish had come to coat it in asphalt, a Victorian commode disguised as a chest of drawers, a set of Elizabethan linen, and a dog from the late eighteenth century someone had had the foresight to stuff and mount on a mahogany stand. Then silver salvers, gold chalices, a single piece of moon no bigger than a sugar cube, the death-mask of an Egyptian king, and a discoloured exercise book showing the original draft of a poem by Thomas Chatterton. Maybe Jim would be in a glass case of his own one day as an example of *Homo Constantly Erectus*.

His destination had been the museum café all along. Its doorway was adjacent to Chatterton's notebook. The café was small, cramped with oak tables and, at this time of day, three-quarters empty. He took a table in the corner next to a small window criss-crossed by iron bars. Escape. They'd had Old Sumatrans here in later years, too, his thick and sticky with two sugars. Through the barred window he could see the main road curving back towards the hospital and, beyond it, the wooded slopes in whose nest the town had been scattered. Through the town's middle ran the broad, ugly river crossed by a series of ill-designed metal bridges. Just half a dozen people sat in the café on three tables holding indistinct conversations. Low mumbles to a nodding of heads or twisting of sugar-bowls. The waitress in this instance was familiar to him: a short, dark-haired young woman with a stud through one nostril. She swung to his table with her pad, wrote down his request and swung away to a side-room. Jeans below a striped pinafore. He wanted to sleep with her, then wanted to apologise for thinking of it. Jim could dream of bed with anyone. Peeling back with layers of imagination the layers of her tight clothing. Could have suckled her like Romulus. Wolf and child. He knew it was going to be one of the last fantasies to die down. Maybe they'd have to subdue it with a surgical mallet. Returning, she clattered his cup and saucer on to the table, then flashed resentment as a customer on the other side of the small room called for more seed-cake. Miriam would have been here with him on Saturdays checking her list, reminding him to tuck in his shirt, then going on to suggest – between the ticking of talcum and tea-bags – that he rarely made an effort to smarten up when he was in her company. He'd have shrugged, wanting to say, 'Of course I don't' in one of his does-anything-really-matter voices. In those days he'd have been preoccupied with the faces of coffee-drinkers, the swank of the punk waitress's jeans, her tawny ankles wriggling in dreams beside his face, and would gradually have adopted the posture of a private eye: hands dug into his cheeks, cigarette hanging from his lips, a squint, his hair uncombed and somehow beyond therapy, his face unshaven for the day.

A man wearing a yellow balaclava and a smeared grey raincoat had appeared in the doorway. He hovered there for a moment or two before coming to Jim with a scowl and thumping his fists against the table. His face loomed forward. Jim looked into his coffee.

'Well?' His deep voice was being subdued by its throatful of wool.

Picking up his spoon, Jim sprinkled two sugars into the black liquid and stirred, following procedures he'd learnt in his dealings with lunacy. The man was repeatedly opening and closing his left fist, making the bones within snap one against the other.

'Well?'

Jim glanced up at the man, whose tired eyes were unsquarely framed by the balaclava, and who now proceeded to sit down and push his plastic-covered arms across the table.

'I suppose you think it's all one big game, don't you, eh? Sitting there with your coffee, not a care in the world. Well, let me tell you this, sunshine.'

Jim would have picked up his coffee had it not been so far from his mouth. 'Tell me what?'

'Oh, it speaks then. It *can* speak. Well, well, well. Had the person what's looking at you not seen it with his own two eyes, he wouldn't have believed it. What do you make of that, eh? You sit in here bold as brass, and mark my words harebrain, no one's going to lift a finger to help you out of this one. No siree. I've buggered you good and proper. And I've a mate waiting out on the steps with orders to capture you if you try to get away. Tell me how you're feeling about that, big boy. Eh? Eh?'

Jim was glancing past the man in the hope of attracting someone's attention, but the three groups of two had huddled closer together and the waitress was still in the side-room cutting, he presumed, a second slice of seed-cake. The man with the balaclava suddenly swung to his right to obscure Jim's view.

'I'd ask you – kindly mind – I'd ask you to pay more attention to the subject in hand, my boy. Namely myself, my friend and the information we've managed to gather together, as you might say. We know the score, old matey. We've sussed the whole thing out. We are *in the know*, my friend and I – a friend who is at this very moment brushing up his violent tendencies out there on the steps. He don't care who he bashes, believe me. He'll bash anybody, will my friend, but he's been looking forward especially to giving you a bashing, a right rare old bashing, and there ain't no escape. *Ain't!*'

Jim stared at the top button of the man's raincoat, which had pulled the waterproofing so tight that the collar was digging into the grey flesh at his neck. 'Look, would you like a coffee? If you don't fancy one, perhaps you'd mind leaving me alone for a moment.'

The man withdrew his arms. 'Oh. So it's *polite* now is it? He's being polite. He's trying to wriggle out of it by way of etiquette. We know about the ways of etiquette me and my friend. We know how people uses it to weedle out of their rightful punishments. But let me warn you, etiquette's of no use whatsoever where my violent friend is concerned. He likes bashing. He looks forward to bashing, and as far as I know there's nothing that would stop him from carrying out a bashing he found to be necessary. Which, in this case, you might say, he most certainly does. Having thought the matter through he said to me this morning – he said he'd never come across someone who so rightfully deserved to be as severely bashed as your good self. No, I won't have a *coffee* as you call it. I've heard all about your types and their coffees. Think you help turn the world, don't you, eh? Let's see what you have to say once justice has been meted out, once my friend what's out there has given full reign to his inexhaustible tendencies for 'orrible violence. Let's see who turns the world then, eh?'

As Jim looked a little higher the man began to chuckle, though it was sound without substance – a chuckle *necessary*, but with no commitment to itself. The depth of the chuckle resonated through the small room but still no one would look in Jim's direction and the punk waitress, having deposited a plate of seed-cake in front of an elderly customer, swanked back into the side-room. The man's eyes were filling with tears.

'When I thinks of it. The times me and my friend have had and some of the people what he has bashed. Good times, my old china. Good times. Now let me see. What have we here in this fine plastic bag? Hmmm. Fags, I could do with a fag myself. And what's this? *The Blue Kiosk*, I see, into readin' and learnin' are we? One of them book types. My friend – he's not into reading at all. He's too busy applying nameless violence on to the bodies of the guilty, and I hate to say it old mate but you're on the bloody list.

Right on it. At the top as a matter of fact. Number one. You are there in black and white. Deserving Of Violence. That's the heading on my friend's list. He loves best of all grabbing blokes' hairstyles and pushing his fist into their mouths. Don't suppose you'd like *that* very much.' The area of balaclava around his mouth was becoming wet. His eyes suddenly gleamed and his voice softened. 'Course, gi's a fag and I might be persuaded to have a word with my friend and dissuade him from those 'orrible practices, and believe me they are 'orrible, most, most 'orrible. Blood, teeth, swollen balls, eyes dangling on stalks, cheeks all ripped up. He can be really nasty. But then, a fag or better still a packet of fags could – if you like – pay a fine and defer the sentence. What say you then – old matey? Tell me the news. Open your gob and speak when you're spoken to.'

Running the tip of his tongue round his teeth, Jim took the bag away from the man, pulled out the cigarettes and gave them to him.

'Why didn't you just say so?'

'Thank you heaps, brother, fellow human, blokey after my own heart. In view of these fags here I will have a word with my friend out there, though he may need some persuading. Once he gets a sniff of a bugger's blood he don't like being disappointed. But I'll do my best.' He was climbing to his feet and shaking Jim's hand. 'Now, if I may make so bold, I'd like to wish you a very good morning and offer you the salutations of one gentleman to another. If I should ever come across you again I'll be sure to have another word with you, assuming, of course, my friend's in the frame of mind for words at all, which he frequently ain't. He'd sooner grab your testicles and nut your bonce, my friend. He ain't what you'd call cultural. He prefers to call a spade a spade. Or better still, whack you with one. That's providing you haven't any fags to give him. He loves a fag. He'd sell his gran for a fag. And may I observe you're looking a bit peaky? May I observe that? I'm sure my friend would agree we're doing you a good turn by taking these here fags away from you, especially since it means in the long run you aint' going to end up being carelessly wallpapered to the pavement. Once he's finished his violence some of our acquaintances have to be paint-scraped up, believe me. Paint-scraped. Now, if you'll excuse me, I'll be running along. Not that I will be running because that's just a saying isn't it? My friend has no patience with sayings. If a bloke comes out with one he's as likely to bash them as anything else. It would be a brave man who'd go up to my friend and say "Warm for the time of year" or "Good day old fellow how are you?" Not that they would because he 'ates everyone but me and puts them off from a hundred yards. 'Ates them. In fact, I've never seen a chap with more 'atred for mankind than he's got.' He leaned forward, placing his yellow mouth close to Jim's ear. 'So mind what you're doing if you spot the old bastard in the street.'

Standing up and waggling the pack of cigarettes at Jim, the man turned and left the café, chuckling to himself. Jim still had a pack in his pocket. He had turned pink around the cheeks but no one was bothering to take any notice of him. Drinking his old Sumatran in one go, he ordered another and lit a cigarette. Through the window he saw the balaclava man hurrying up the road with another, slightly shorter, balaclava man at his side.

ii

I've been thinking of Oswald, particularly of subsequent times when Jane came to believe he was pustule-free. She was picking her way along the top of the wall beside us, arms held out like a tightrope walker, her overly plump legs a drawback he'd chosen to ignore. She was the girl going out with him, according to stories he'd put about, yet she always had me along as referee, supervisor to their afternoons, So wrapped up in analysis of her was Oswald that he missed the moment she hung back, pulled her ears and poked out her tongue at him. Had he seen her, his life might have become further diseased and he could have ended up hating members of the congregation who now kneel before him for wine and wafers. Peace be with you, Oswald. Jane was more bountiful than Laurinda, which is why she was second on his list. Third place was still open to offers. Peggy Mount could have filled it. And let's remember the error of his suggestion that Jane should slim down. It made her grumpy, persuaded her to walk along the wall rather than at his side. The situation led one to consider the moments which take place when we aren't looking: the clues we miss, and how different our outlook would be if, as they say, we had eyes in the backs of our heads and could catch the gigglers, the infidels, the insincere – though it would mess up Shakespearian plays, undermine their dramatic irony.

We reached the quarry. I was smoking Gold Leaf. Oswald stood at the far side, dim in the quarry's shadow, his nose almost completely blocked. Maybe if he hadn't tried to overcome this in front of Jane the afternoon would have taken a more successful turn. Each time either of us caught sight of her navy blue dress our throats seized up. Then there were snatches of her turkey thighs, which she may have been unpeeling on purpose, who knew with talked-about girls like her? No sense of sugar, spice or all things nice. The corners of her eyes twinkled as if with frozen teardrops, taking us by surprise that green and wicked afternoon as she suggested we undress her and tie her to a tree with vine – only, of course, the thinnest and most pliable tugged from the twigs of a nearby tree. She turned out a Basset's Jelly Baby. Were those breasts or just puppy fat? Even as we accomplished the final bind I believe we were wondering how to unknot desires set up in us by the idea; and anyway, it took just moments for us to be bored by her. Then there were unspoken prayers between us that she would free herself and dress again so we could imagine her instead. This was a day when much apology was owed to God by Oswald. Oh, but what a beautiful face had misled us! She giggled there against the trunk, her arms raised, vine pressing into an excessive abdomen, her breast tissue no more seductive than that of the overweight boy in our class, Clive Stickletrench (his name an added burden to natural obesity). Almost all overweight boys in school were called Stickletrench, while slim, handsome devils had slim, handsome names. Oswald wandered away from the tree holding a tissue to his nose. His clothes had obviously been bought by a mother with an eye on the traditional values of neatness and Christianity and an excessive trust in the use of starch, turning him crisp if not a little dazzling. Sorry, but that's the truth. Jane was waiting there like Siamese Tinkerbells: our first joint glimpse of an unclothed girl. At the time of her undressing, the sun had been shining and the wood had been a cathedral of birdsong, but gradually the afternoon became masked by grey cloud and, had she not been watching us, I suspect we would have crept away for a conference, since she was becoming ratty with our indecisive messing about and may have been making up tales of assault to tell her short but beefy father. Oswald would confess later he'd read somewhere that girls were like that – making up nasty things about you if you didn't do what they were asking. And to make things worse, it was often necessary to unveil several psychological layers of the girl in question, since she would sometimes ask you to do the reverse of what she really wanted; which is why, when your life is half through, it becomes all buckled up, and why you may turn your attention to higher things, things which don't need constant re-evaluation.

Attempting to placate the situation and urged on by Oswald I took off my own clothes and rested against Jane's body, closing my eyes briefly to kiss her closed mouth. Oswald, my friend, was it absolutely necessary for you to applaud? I assure you it was Jane's idea and not mine that the vines should be untied and then re-tied with me on the inside against her. Thank you for your help in achieving this, but I'm still irritated at how you sneaked away once the job was done, especially since Jane found much to amuse herself in both the structure of my body and those Ruyard Kipling motifs on my discarded underwear. It took some time for us to struggle free. And what pieces of body touched pieces of body in the attempt. And there were sheep, I remember, bleating in an emerald field somewhere below us. Had you been with me, Oswald, I suspect you too would have experienced the awful loneliness which came with our embarrassment and broken conversation. There are songs and hymns ringing through the cathedrals of our lives which we can't quite catch and are suspicious of. Maybe we are finally persuaded instead to concentrate on the simple clicking of our shoes against an ecclesiastical floor.

iii

'So. You've been making a dash for it.'

Jim looked away from *The Blue Kiosk*. Miranda pulled back a chair and settled herself opposite him. 'It's a good job I found you first. Sister's been ringing me at home. Really angry, she is. I mean, quite demented. So much for my day off, and it's your fault.'

'Go back home. I just wanted coffee. Real coffee.'

'She's been on to the police, social bloody services. Tried to get hold of your wife but she's not in. Gave me the third degree as if it was my fault. And here you are.'

'How did you know I'd be up here?'

'I didn't. I told the old rat I'd have a drive round thinking I'd do some shopping at the same time. Parked just up there. Bought a few things, had a look round just in case, then came in for a drink. I got bored, as a matter of fact. Didn't think for a minute you'd be hanging about here.' She was wearing a black, knee-length coat over black jeans and jumper. The unpinned dark hair was falling round her shoulders.

He placed *The Blue Kiosk* opened but cover-upwards on the table. 'It was a quest if you like. I wanted to see how far I could get.'

'You're mad. I'd better take you back while you're still vertical.'

'Oh, don't fuss. Have a coffee first. Have an Old Sumatran.'

She leaned forwards rubbing her eyes. 'Yeah, and get myself the chop.'

'Look, there's no hurry. I haven't run away altogether. Fancied a break from it, that's all.' Jim waved his hand towards the waitress who'd just delivered fresh coffee to a table opposite. Ordered a third Old Sumatran for himself and one for Miranda, whose nose was twitching as if she were a rabbit in a spring meadow.

'Just one then, and back we go.'

'Why do nurses always say things like that? *Back we go.* We happen to be talking about my body, my ailment, and my life.'

'I'm just trying to help you.'

Jim laughed. 'No you're not. Probably you're just squandering a need for what they call meaningful relationships by wielding power over weak men, viz: me.'

Thrusting her spoon into the cane sugar she lowered her chin and spoke in a whisper. 'You've been practising that, haven't you? Anyway, whatever else I may have done I haven't been personal. Why get at me just because you're annoyed?'

'You've got it all wrong. I *want* you to be personal. Whenever you say things like "Back we go" it makes me feel I don't exist.'

The room had become noticeably smaller since Jim's arrival, though even he had ceased being excited about it. Why rage against the inevitable? He looked at her delicately-veined eyelids and smiled.

'I'm sorry. I suppose I'm getting a bit carried away.'

The superficial strength which had been with him had begun to drain, for some reason, through his wrists and hands. For once he was finding it tricky to raise his replenished cup or correctly manipulate his cigarette. Maybe he'd die of all these watercolour thoughts. Or Miranda would want to thrash the romance out of him, turn him practical till the third crowing of the cock when she'd implore him to relinquish things of the spirit, those harmonic undersongs not open to examination.

She screwed up her eyes to take a sip, lowered the cup thoughtfully, and swallowed. 'OK, OK. I know you're under a bit of strain. I just wanted . . . Well, I thought it might be better if I took you back sooner rather than later.' Now she was playing with her ear, squeezing its fleshy lobes between thumb and first finger. 'That is, unless you can think of anything you want to do first. A brief swansong, shall we say?'

'What sort of thing?'

She shrugged. 'Oh, I don't know. Maybe you want to feed ducks, have your palm read, or listen to Julie Andrews LPs. I can't say. I'm not privy to your dreams.'

'Pretty swift change of tune isn't it?'

'Perhaps I was overdoing it just now, barging in here the way I did.'

'That's all right. I haven't been in the best of humours myself. Let's forget it.'

She was tapping her cup, washing its contents from side to side. 'This coffee's dreadful. It must be full of caffeine.'

'Of course it's full of caffeine. That's why I like it.'

'Very bad for you.'

'Some of the best things are bad for you, ultimately.'

A change of mood crossed her face like the shadow of a cloud. Jim had linked his ankles under the table and was stifling a yawn.

'Listen,' she said. 'I shouldn't be saying this because it's not the best thing to do but perhaps it wouldn't do much harm if you came over to my place for elevenses or something. Yeah, elevenses. I haven't got much there but then I don't suppose you're very hungry. In the meantime, if you think of anything else you'd like to do we can take it from there. How would that grab you?'

'I don't mind. As long as you're not being maternal.'

She was irritated at this. 'No, of course not. It's not easy dealing with you, you know. Part of me wants to do the right thing and the other part . . . Well, I can't blame you for not wanting to go straight back into that place.'

Jim tried bunching up his chin and lips like he'd practised in mirrors, but wasn't sure he was doing it well enough. 'I don't really understand your swings of attitude, but if it's no trouble, I'd really like to come back with you. What do you usually do on your days off?'

'Oh, read, do the shopping. Have a sleep if I've been up late the night before.'

'If you're tired we can just forget it.'

'It was my idea for God's sake. I'm no martyr. I *want* you to come.'

Bitter coffee at the back of his throat – a taste bringing back sunshades, lazy afternoons, warm pavements, a breeze making whirlpools out of paper scraps. He'd loved till his senses hurt with it, though his passions had swung too widely for him to be declared a dependable person. All the same, he had reaped a few dreams, dreams to snuffle through in the thick of night. Miranda was playing with her serviette, tearing it into two, then four pieces. It won't come. Any of it. Despite this wringing of consciousness. A discrepancy in the imagination, undermining substance, these walls nearing the tables by degrees, the barred window distorting under the weight of so much sky, and, out of touch – a breath, a rhythm of syllables, twists of incense, old sea-songs.

Miranda insisted on paying the bill. As she was talking to the waitress, Jim pulled himself to his feet. She caught the tail-end of his struggle and laughed to herself, touching his shoulder and leading him to the door. Her car was on a meter a few yards along a sidestreet. Jim rested his arms against the roof while she opened the doors. The drive took them over the farthest bridge to the east of town, then on through avenues of limes. Houses and hedges and pedestrians slipped against the windows in streaks of green and beige till, turning a corner, the car pulled up at a rank of three-storey Edwardian houses, most of them with dormer windows in the attic. Miranda pointed upwards to one with blue curtains.

'I suppose I'll have to push you up the stairs.'

'Yes, of course.'

'Sorry. I didn't think.'

'Don't apologise. All this time you've haven't been apologising for yourself. Why start now?'

He followed her to the green front door, waited while she rummaged for her key, then stepped behind her into a small dark hall smelling of cats, casserole and damp wallpaper. A chill of recognition twisted through him which, after a moment, he dismissed as déjà vu. At the top of the first two flights of stairs was a pair of silent, numbered doors painted white. A third, much narrower set of stairs led from the landing to the purple door of her attic flat. He'd refused her help, though the effort of pretending had become an almost unbearable weight by the time they reached the top of this last flight. Once inside, she suggested he sit down while she fetched some orange juice. In the white-painted living room the down-slope of the roof met the horizontals of the dormer creating sharp triangles too low for him to walk under. Against the wall were bookshelves, a cane waste-paper basket packed with balls of wool, a small desk. In the centre of the room lying diagonally, was a large black-and-white striped rug. The floorboards it partially covered had been varnished. In the corner stood an old-fashioned record player on an oak side-table. Above it hung a reproduction art deco mirror, the frame on one side moulded into the shape of a dancing woman in twenties' clothing. On closer inspection, Jim noticed that the blue curtains were in fact flecked with white butterflies. On the dining table stood a large bowl of pot pourri whose sweet scent was filling the room. A scallop-shaped three-piece suite in dark green had been arranged close to the side and end walls. Ranked along a pine mantelpiece above one of the scalloped chairs were a couple of dozen paperweights of different colours and sizes. This snoopiness, like Sherlock. The swift assessment of other people's lives. Among the furnishings lay a mood of anxiety as if Miranda had been unhappy here. She'd thrown her coat on a large floor-cushion just inside the door. Two records out of their sleeves were lying by the record player. Then, more déjà vu: perfume from the pot pourri, the rattle of windows in wind, or maybe the empty milk bottle on the windowsill. Cockerels all. A pair of black tights had been left hanging by their toes from the mantelpiece, two ink-blue paperweights holding them in place. He sat on the sofa. It rolled back against the wall, causing his feet to lift. From the kitchen he could hear the hum of her fridge, a rattle of glasses, Miranda talking to herself. He had taken a dislike to the balls of wool, the pair of knitting needles lying crossed on the dining table just behind the bowl of pot pourri, the old cup on the right arm of the sofa with dried specks of tea at its rim, the fluffed plumes of jumpers seen in the partially-opened drawer of a stripped pine chest.

Miranda appeared at his side with two glasses of juice.

'Would you like something to eat then? I could heat

up some soup or there's mushroom salad from yesterday. Or baked beans.'

He took the glass she was holding out to him. 'Do you have bread? I wouldn't mind some toast. Just toast.'

'What? Nothing on it?'

'No. Nothing.'

'One slice or two?'

'One please.'

'Right, I'll have a breather, then make it for you.' Taking a sip from her glass she placed it on a small table beside the sofa, waved him along with the flat of her hands, and sat down in his place, crossing her legs and leaning back. 'Do you like the flat? You haven't said.'

Jim looked around himself. 'Yes, I was just thinking. It's –'

'I've been really lucky. The landlord was a patient on our ward. I don't pay more than half the rent I should. He's a lovely man. Comes round every week to check I'm all right.'

Jim swallowed the juice he'd been swishing round his teeth in the hope of changing the taste in his mouth. 'Huh, that's pretty –'

'And being here makes me feel completely secure. I couldn't live on the ground floor. The other tenants are all quiet as mice. The landlord prefers older people on the whole. Sometimes during the day, if you're on the pavement outside, you can see them all looking through their windows like guardians. I can't have bumped into any of them more than a couple of times.'

Jim threw his head back to laugh but changed his mind. 'Reminds me of –'

'And if there's ever a problem, a blocked drain or

something, I just give the landlord a ring and there's someone here the next day. He's more of a father than anything else.' Her free hand had come to rest on Jim's knee. She patted it. 'Anyway. Have you given any thought to your swansong? Is there something you'd really really like to do while you have the chance? All I'd ask is that you don't tell anyone. I wouldn't want to get myself into trouble.'

'My lips are –'

'So we'll see to your toast and then I'll be at your disposal.'

Jim took a little more juice and leaned forward to look at his shoelace.

'*Thanks*, Miranda,'

'So what do you think?'

'It's a difficult one. I feel I need more time.'

She had uncrossed her legs and was standing up, using one hand on his shoulder as leverage. 'Chew it over while I'm in the kitchen.'

'OK.' He watched in fascination as she reached forward to ruffle his hair.

'You're a strange man, Jim. Quite, quite strange.'

'Thank you.'

'Are you sure you want nothing on it? Strawberry jam? Marmite? Peanut butter?'

'Quite sure.'

She went to the kitchen, leaving him to think things through. Immediately he was remembering a violet sunset with trees against it like strokes of charcoal, and the silences of Laura at the hub of him. They'd been walking since tea-time among iron-age tombs on the cold common, watching out for shooting stars – several times she had touched his arm just as the tails of them were being extinguished. Both were hoping reports of aliens landing in Yugoslavia had some basis in fact. There was a need for some objective group to mumble *Well, love-a-duck*, when told the full, complex history of the planet over schnapps. The cheek he brushed with the back of his finger was cold, though blushed violet too. With a sense of needing to save things up, he looked at her profile sparingly. Yes. They wandered back to a clearing with a view of the vale where the car was parked, the windscreen also violet, her cobweb skirt faintly coloured too, soft legs below its crumpled hem, her hair, the blue of her eyes turning a momentary sunset. Then those laps of belly-skin as she lifted her T-shirt for a laugh, blushed navel, immoral kisses as if God were nearby keeping score. Jim recalled a brief discussion about how one would classify Rolf Harris if one was forced into it: a singing painter or a painting songster? Laura was trying to picture him hoeing leeks and couldn't. Perhaps it was madness, but with his hand to her face it was as if Jim had missed touching it all along. These insanity poems conjured for the long night ahead. Fairy tales. She figured fidelity could be a traitor in itself – the accomplishment of dreams wounding the innocent but a denial of them just further wounding the already wounded, her T-shirt opening as she hung forward, a general knowledge quiz on the radio hosted by someone whose voice was so familiar they couldn't remember his name. She was first to answer the one about *Tristram Shandy*. All double Dutch to him. They slunk down as a group of night scouts walked by wearing rucksacks and carrying torches. Coming unstuck. And over the next hour they saw a tramp with a plastic sheet tucked under his arm, the eyes of a fox, the shadows of a pair of villains, and then heard in the vale hymns from a distant choir. He smoked to avoid issues. She wanted to show him where she'd been bitten by a gnat in a crease of white skin at her waist. The violet darkened to black. She was becoming a shadow and moved as a shadow in the driving seat, surprising him with her hand, teasing that Jesuit conscience till she was almost nothing but fragrance, a cool of mouth, a rustle of legs. Might turn out gods wanted what people wanted for themselves, then there'd be much snapping of unspent fingers at the gates, hearing first-hand of opportunities sent which were turned away. Coming bloody unstuck. Three out of ten on European capitals. Michael Aspel. Laura had remembered it eventually. She drove away down the rough track out onto the narrow lane, braking hard by the fingerpost to avoid running over a badger. The branches of overhead trees became cobwebs in the headlights. Tired of fruitless wooing, she announced she was heading for the sea. He attached his safety belt and wound his seat back a little. But then . . . the question hadn't been answered. There were too many possibilities. Butterflies. Blackberries. Bookshops on summer afternoons. Fishing but not catching anything in Scottish lochs. Miranda was singing. Eventually she came in with the plate of toast and placed it in his lap. 'I've just thought of an ideal swansong.'

Jim's mouth curled down.

Where his ailment had taken away energy and inventiveness, Miranda took over, adopting positions he would normally have chosen himself and moving where he was unable to as they reached an uneasy harmony of one skin with another – Jim's the poorest, his bones like rocks hidden close to shore, Miranda deep and supple by contrast, her skin the colour, the taste of almonds, well-formed, no wastage, her mouth opening in proximity to his and in those pupils his own taut face reflected, pale, pinched around the nose as if his skin had been shrinking too. Whole narratives of beauty were being put to the test since hand in hand with recent degeneration had come a loss of some previous nobility. Such credence he'd given over the years to his appearance, yet now it was as nothing, leaving exposed the peaks and troughs of self. In view of this, questions arose during long undulation, Miranda above or beside him: was she being kind? Nor could he decide who he was turning infidel to. Since toast, events had taken an inevitable run at him. And wasn't it true that when he was close, really close, to a stranger's body it became more than familiar, all aspects of the common denominator reaching out? A cocktail of senses. A taste of melon-juice in her saliva, his hands roughing her hair, the thump of her heart as she pressed against him, the buckle of sheets, his back pushed down, Miranda's shadow overwhelming him. He listened to the town and to the ticking of her cooker clock and to her quickening breath, too ashamed to look at her much, his head often sideways on the white pillow though his hands reached about her, following her lines, cupping here, dipping there. The bed was almost filling the small bedroom, leaving only enough space for the door to half-open and, elsewhere, an eighteen-inch gap. She meant none of it, probably, and when it was over it wouldn't matter whether she did or not. Pray for a dozen hands to follow her, a number of mouths. He was kissing her shoulder-blade, following her spine with his tongue. Forgive the infidelity of this infidelity. Red toes in his mouth. Sunken belly against her eyelids. Tongue in the crook of her knee. From one point of view he could see the landscape of leg, abdomen, the tip of her nose and a fan of hair against the pillow. Or she would stroke his pelvic bone, the skin there tight, translucent to workings beneath. Here be veins, sinews like tubes of blue neon. And though he was mostly ashamed she seemed to relish it well enough, lying edgewise to brush the hair of this fishbone sternum or kissing the frail muscle of his upper thigh, the white, uncooked pheasant pieces, her arms thrown back, dark hair in the mouths of them, clutching pinpoints of dew, the bloom of her hip, changes in her skin from almond to ivory, ivory to pale rose where fever caught her. A nightmare of skin, sweat, movement. His legs open, hers opening to make room for his head, or closing to catch him there, fruit-wounds, moist kernels spilling out. 'Think of it as physiotherapy,' she was saying – and the beast having the equivalent of a day out in Frinton. He was thinking he might not continue with it even as his mouth reached to lick those wounds. 'Oh Jim, you are a caution.' Tick-tock, fucking cooker clock, her sterterous breathing, the sounds of some gobbling duck-skin, the accidental thump of her thigh against his cheek. Close up, this piece could belong to anyone. Lyrics through his conscience to pass the time, *Ich bin ein Berliner*. Once dreamed of really giving it to Edna in his camp bed, her hair, narratives, poetic constructions running to the floor as Miriam slept and dreamed of ring-tailed Lemurs. Oh he was getting into the swing of it now. If you do it hard enough, refuse to turn back, it eventually comes and you end up wondering what the problem was in the first place. The world's just unspent loving channelled in various ways. The road-sweeper thinks of it each time he pushes his thick broom into gutter cracks – these leaves can be intimate hair. The woman at the podium denouncing Communism may stroke her notes in a particular way, remembering a fascist guy from the night before with his white trousers and bulging chicken breasts in white wine sauce.

Before the end had come she lay beside him breathing heavily, stroking his fringe.

'Are you happy with how your swansong's going?'

Jim brushed the sweat from his breast. 'On the whole I am, but I've been slightly worried you might be putting up with it for my sake.'

She was pressing her breasts against his ribcage. 'It is for your sake, but I'm not putting up with it. There may have been elements of that at first, but I'm having a reasonably good time now. Something about you is quite exhilarating. I think it's those worry lines round your eyes.'

'I don't really believe you. I mean, look at me.'

'And I can't deny there's a kick in knowing I'll be your last. Sorry. I shouldn't say that.'

He kissed the top of her head. 'That's OK. I expect you will be. You can say what you like. I prefer honesty.'

'And do you know something? You're looking better than I've ever seen you. Not such a ghost.' Reaching up, she pecked his mouth, her breasts slipping against his wet chest. 'Don't worry if you can't go right through to the end by the way. I'll . . . Well, I'll give you a hand.'

Jim swallowed. 'Thank you. That might be

necessary. I feel fine at the moment but maybe it's just fooling itself.'

She changed position. 'You mean *this*?'

Jim raised his chin. 'Yes. *That.*'

She made a series of flicking movements with the thing between her fingers. 'And there I was thinking I might have stumbled on an unrecorded cure. Don't tell me. You've been thinking of home.'

'No. Innisfree. That's what I've been thinking about.'

'What's that?'

'Oh it's the name of a place somewhere. Probably in Ireland. Lakes, swans, peace of mind. Stuff like that.'

'I wouldn't mind if you were thinking about it. Home, I mean. Your wife perhaps?'

'No. Honest. And I think I'd be happier if you didn't keep bringing it up.'

'Only twice. I wouldn't say that was overdoing it.'

'Sorry then.'

She moved back and looked at him. 'I feel quite sad for her in a way.'

'Who?'

'Your wife. I mean, here we are on your penultimate day and you're dragging strange women into bed. Distressing, really, isn't it?'

'I shouldn't worry. She has a boyfriend.'

'Oh. So you're taking some kind of revenge before you go.'

'What do you mean? That's a bloody awful thing to say. And why are you bringing all this up now? We're only two-thirds of the way through.'

'I can tell by the tone of your voice that you're angry about her. I was putting two and two together. And you must care. I always think that if you're angry enough over someone it means you really care about them.'

Jim rolled her over, slipped down and rested his head between her breasts. 'Earlier on you were saying you'd do what you could to help me this morning. Perhaps you could make a start by shutting up about my wife.'

With the nub of her palm, Miranda had pushed her breast so that its nipple lay against his lips. 'If that's what you want. I was just interested. People fascinate me.' Then, unplucking herself from his mouth, she pushed him flat and began to explore his thinning reaches. He studied the ceiling, composed limericks, made his apologies to Laura. Then craned his neck to review Miranda's downward progress.

'Maybe you should die of *this*,' she said.

Jim was tucked above her, watching the shifts of sunlight which illuminated the room then pulled back leaving rumours of grey. A bus was whining down the lime-bordered road. She was raising strands of hair and letting them fall, her free hand against the small of his back. He could smell her warm skin, the tangled bedclothes which had been thrown back to give him air, cool him down.

Miranda's voice: 'We didn't practise safe sex.'

'Sorry.'

'No. I'm not blaming you. Neither of us mentioned anything.'

Jim was yawning. 'I thought about it while you . . . Too late anyway.'

'Call me irresponsible, but there's always something about life which improves when it's not safe. Don't you agree?'

He nodded, noticing at the same time how his cheek was sticking to her chest. 'Other than that, Miranda, I'd just like to say –'

Her hand came over his mouth. 'You're not going to thank me are you? Or give one of those Grandstand summaries: *Well, it's been a great sporting occasion and I for one thoroughly enjoyed it?* With things the way they are I don't suppose anyone would be the least bit surprised that we came to bed rather than taking a country walk.'

Jim lifted his head till his cheek unstuck, then settled it back into position. Outside, a screech of tyres and the sound of a horn were followed by someone with a deep voice shouting, 'Oi. Watch where you're going!'

'It's interesting,' she continued, 'that as a race we hardly ever admit that making love for the sake of it is a nice thing. When was the last time you saw a rabbit going to a psychotherapist? I mean, it's not some awful sin and neither is it the best thing on earth. Just something pleasant, like the thought of a salmon sandwich or Black Forest Gâteau. Of course, if you're in love then it takes on greater significance and that's all well and good. I'm not advocating people should do it willy-nilly. Only that they shouldn't compose guilt-ridden soliloquies if it happens. We wanted it. We've undertaken it. What could be simpler?'

Like the wheels of a gaming machine, Jim's mind reeled with possible answers, though his final conclusions were as unworthy of mention as two melons and a bell. Her left leg had crooked itself against the right to make a rough figure 4. Without moving he managed to look sideways and down at the same time to watch the slight dome of her abdomen and, further on, almond thigh-slopes, where his fingers were playing like children in snow.

'I'm glad this has happened,' she was saying. 'And though it wasn't the most memorable experience of its kind, I suspect, having made allowances, that at one time you were really rather good at it.'

'Well, you know. I don't feel I've . . . '

'Being good at it doesn't always happen naturally, even if you're in love. Alex does it as though he's been put on a football field with fifteen ferrets and told not to let any of them cross the touchline. Coffee? No Old Sumatran I'm afraid. Just instant.'

'Instant is fine.'

'I suppose when you're at home you and your wife make it with filters and everything.'

'No.'

'I hate that. The process looks and smells wonderful, but the coffee's always cold by the time it reaches you. Roll over then, and I'll make some.'

Jim moved onto his back to watch as Miranda climbed over him, shuffled off the bed, yawned, opened the door as far as it would go and squeezed out. Somehow Laura was admonishing him from dark corners, her grin matching the grin of a stuffed clown which had been keeping watch from the windowsill. In the kitchen, a clattering of spoons, Miranda humming part of the *Messiah*. The ceiling trembled as if he were watching it through water. He fancied he heard something of a tom-cat in her movements and, in the lower scales of her humming, some of the tone and melodrama of Miriam's voice. Now she would be deciding whether raw cane or granulated would be best. UHT, semi-skimmed or full cream? The oak, plastic or cork tray? Apostle, motorway or silver-plated spoons? Mug or cup? If cup, Worcester, Habitat or the ones free with the thousand gallons of petrol? If mug, the Lions of Longleat, I Hate Mondays or white with zig-zag blue stripes? Those with least choice must find living a more splendoured thing. If Miranda's bare feet rested in one position for more than a few seconds then she was having to unstick them from the lino just as Jim had unstuck his cheek from her breast, a breast which had swayed as if full of sunflower oil. Pretty damn suspicious, isn't it, a soliloquy lasting more or less the same time as it takes to boil a kettle? The beast had taken on weight. No longer spent, but not yet sprightly. Curling at his thigh like a mischievous child planning a raid on fairy cakes in the pantry. Yes, something of Miriam here, as if her phantom had taken up residence. He retrieved the covers, twisted on to his side, lay his palms under his cheek and tucked up his knees.

Usually we were in a parked car, both reclining on the bri-nylon seats, the handbrake between us, her liquid crystal clock reminding me of the time, strands of cobweb skirt as cobwebs in the corner of my eye. Yes. One time there were illuminated cranes swinging girders through half-darkness and grounded office men peeking through the car's moist windows, men swanking with grey portfolios. We were miracles of indecision, Laura and I, and somewhere along the line I couldn't bear her simplicity. She was laughing over a lady in a Crosse & Blackwell coat who was selling newspapers under the Roman archway. Went on to say she'd read somewhere of an exercise for removing the pain of people's demands on the soul, imagining those demands as maggots with firm gums gripping the affected part. All you had to do was rip them away and hand them back to the person concerned saying, 'There you are. Have your pain back.' If they refused then the affected person should insist. So I used to pull the beast from my chest, but couldn't decide who to give it to. Perhaps it should have been myself. What Laura knew didn't cover that possibility. And the Roman arch had its own raven standing dark up there, like Satan taking comfort from the moon. Laura thought they only had ravens at the Tower, so perhaps it was a starling after all. Still, it was fun to conjecture, fun conjecturing in the steams of her unconsummated car.

The switch of the kettle clicked out. He heard water being poured among Miranda's *Hallelujah, Hallelujah, ha-llayee-lu-yahhhh.*

Then she was pushing back into the bedroom with a metal tray, two coffees and a plate of biscuits.

'Always makes me peckish. Doesn't it you?'

There it was again: an echo of Miriam in the rhythms of her voice. Jim sat up to receive his coffee. Miranda remained cross-legged above the covers to drink hers, resting her elbows on splayed knees. As soon as she'd finished she slid to the floor and pulled a pad and a box of pastel crayons from under the bed.

'I'm going to draw you.'

Climbing on to the far end of the bed, she resumed her cross-legged position and lay the pad on her knees, setting the crayon box at her side. For half a minute she stared at him, leaning her head first one way, then another.

'Sit up just a bit more. I want the blanket to be on a line with your belly button.'

Jim did as he was told, then lit a cigarette. Since his arrival the spire of the nearby church had come closer still. He followed its beige cone down to the top of Miranda's head. Her breasts were splayed against the lower edge of the pad. Under the pad itself, cream shadows had gathered among her thighs.

'All your ribs are visible. It's absolutely great.'

He looked down. Indeed they were. And this cigarette was the best he'd ever had. Miranda was now all cream and gold, top teeth biting lower lip, one eye closing each time she looked at him. Suddenly she raised the pad and turned over the next sheet.

'Sorry Jim. It wasn't quite right. Do you think you could lower the blanket a bit more?'

'There?'

'No. Further. That's it. Keep going. And more. Ah, there we are.'

Keeping his head as still as possible, Jim glanced down. Yes, it was as he'd suspected. He drew on his cigarette with a heightened sense of urgency. She was asking him to keep his eyes on her. He obeyed. Those squashed red toes. Recently they'd been in his mouth. Her calves clean-shaven and somehow luminous. The fullness of those resting breasts, a vein visible beneath the surface of the one on the right, its nipple still dark and swollen. Nurturing her baby, she'd been. Deep below the pad he followed the convergence of skins to darker brushstrokes where hair would be. Lithe, is it? And moistened by his mouth. There are no beginnings. Just an overlapping of this with that. Time most of all. No beginnings. The skin at her neck a faint shade of rose and covered in goosebumps; a blush on her cheeks; hair a puff of dark smoke. The movement of her right hand was bold, as if she were establishing some rough outline, her eyes roving from the pad to the top of his head, down to the blanket-line, and back again.

'Could you open your legs more? I hate thighs all

bunched up. Great. Keep them like that.'

The beast unceremoniously slipped into this new crevasse and wouldn't come out of its own accord.

'God, your eyes are incredible, Jim. Powerful, know what I mean?' A cloud which had been dimming the room slid away. Her shadow fell across the bed.

'Yes. The eyes of a fox at night.'

Remembering a moon; Laura; the loving of the understood and the loving of the yet to be understood. He can't smoke quick enough. Laura in moon, her skin turning treacle. Laura in beaten gold. With every sentence he would say her name. *Laura*. Listen to her breathing in those shadows of the car. Parked by the sea at last. A necklace of moon against its dark skin. The steady crush of water on pebbles, a scrabble as it retreated to the deeps. She said they couldn't go on talking in cars for the rest of their lives so she was going away – away sounding a terrible, fantastic place to be headed. Sea-lions. Russian fishermen in thick socks. Crabs in pans of boiling water. He didn't touch her because she was the thing he wanted. He'd touched everything else only to watch it decompose, so he tried not touching her. Like a bird released into the sky with no message on a Sunday morning. Maybe it would return of its own free will. Further along, the lights of the seaside town were bobbing on the water. Then there were tales she told of its whisky-golden poet boozing on oaken settles, her legs, hushed together in a second cobweb skirt, taking on blushes of the moon. From bushes behind the car, someone coughed; followed by broken laughter as if the cougher hadn't wanted to be caught loving by the sea. 'Such children we have in us all the time,' she said. Then she rolled over with nothing to add except a reiteration of those sea-lion dreams.

'How's it going?'
Miranda leaned back. 'Not too badly at all.'
'I've never been drawn.'
'I love doing it. Love it.'
'Can I see?'
'In a while. You probably won't recognise yourself. I'm trying to make an interpretation rather than an exact image.'
'It's something I've always wanted to do. But I'm useless at it.'
'Oh, it's like everything else. You learn the rules, then break them.'
She smiled in reassurance then curled the tip of her tongue on to her upper lip, twisting the pad to attend more closely to a particular area of the paper – as if men could become golden too, bones beneath an amber skin, muscles creating subtle folds as wind in sand-dunes.
Suddenly she threw the pad aside. He looked at it. Even from this angle, it was evident she'd added a certain grandeur to his failing structure, restored a bloom he hadn't known for a while. The drawing was skilled in perspective and composition. The colours were imaginative, adding opinion to substance. She came to sit at his side, her waist twisting as a mermaid's might. He stared at the abandoned pad wondering what he might say but, thankfully, she rescued him.
'I have a confession to make, Jim.' She took a biscuit, bit into it, then pushed the escaping crumbs

back into her mouth with her little finger. 'The person I mentioned just now. Alex. Thank you for not probing me about it, but I'm afraid I have to bring him up because he's . . . well, relevant. You see, he'll be coming round later and I'd appreciate it if you weren't here when he arrived. He'll probably stay the night. Usually does. Otherwise I'd have suggested you went back to the hospital in the morning.'

'Who is he anyway?'

'He's just a good friend really. His parents and mine own the same company and he's sort of a rising star there. They've got it into their heads we'll get married one day, but I don't think it'll happen. We sleep together, but who doesn't? It's more out of habit than anything else. Anyway, what I'm trying to say is that I think I should take you back soon even though what I really want is for you to stay.'

'Fine. But you don't have to take me.'

'What do you mean?'

'What I said. I don't want you to take me. And don't argue. You did say you'd try to do what I wanted today.'

'But –'

'Look. Nobody knows I'm here but you. Just relax.'

'What is something happens to you on the way back?'

'That's my responsibility, not yours.'

Her fingers were walking along his belly. 'Fair enough. If that's what you want. I'll be seeing you when I come on duty tomorrow anyway. You do understand, don't you? I feel really bad about it but . . .'

He was twisting to the tickle of her fingers. 'Don't

say anything else. I wasn't expecting to stay here despite what's happened. It was just my swansong, remember?'

'Good. Thank you.' Her fingers were straying downwards. 'Do you know something? Drawing really turns me on.'

Jim reached for the pad. 'It's excellent. I love this area of blue here.'

Kneeling either side of his legs, she unhooked the pad from his fingers and threw it against the wall.

'The overall colour-scheme –'

'Shut up and woodle me.'

'Woodle you?'

She was stroking his pubic hair. 'A pet name I have for it. You know what I mean.' She gazed into his eyes. 'Yes, woodle me. Woodle me all afternoon.'

Jim took a deep breath. The beast had popped its head out of the crevasse. 'Yes, well, Miranda. It isn't that I don't want to woodle you . . . '

She shuffled forwards till her thighs were tight against his, then threw her nails forwards, digging them into his abdomen.

'Come on then, Jim boy. Woodle me. Let's not bother with any of that foreplay stuff. We've made love, now let's woodle.'

'You have beautiful shoulders.'

A trail of blood was seeping to the surface of his broken skin.

'I don't want to hear about my shoulders. Just woodling. Look.'

Rising from his belly, her fingers skimmed her own broad thighs, then slithered to her groin. Sniffing, Jim began to stroke her knees. She grasped his left hand and pushed it to her breast. Jim sniffed again. It was a tickle at the back of his nose he was trying to scratch.

'As I said, I *would* like to woodle but I don't think I've . . . '

She took three of his fingers, squeezed them together and held them up. 'Use these,' she said. 'Woodle me with these.'

He was laughing, though the expression of it wouldn't reach his face. Reluctantly he did as he was told. She bounced up and down, circling her fingers at various erogenous zones.

'Deeper, Zhim. Woodle me as if you 'ated me.'

'I think I do hate you, Miranda. And why the French accent? What's come over you?'

'Nothink yet, but you weel if I 'ave anythink to do wiz eet.'

He smiled without conviction, his fingers lone emissaries rather than representatives of his spirit. And in response her hips rose and bore down, rose and bore down. The beast, ignoring his general fatigue, climbed completely from the crevasse and looked around.

'Oh, 'ere eet eez at last,' she said, abandoning one erogenous zone to grapple with it. Jim had been trying to mask his sniffles as breathings-in, but he could sense a pearl of moisture rolling slowly but inexorably down his right nostril till it reached the exit and waited there. Taking his fingers out she loomed forward, wriggled on to him, grasped his chest hair and rolled her hips.

'Oh, I love zee way you do thees, Zhim.'

Putting aside a natural inclination to disclaim responsibility, Jim was reaching with his mouth in an attempt to catch one of her nipples, though this turned into a party game leading him to chuckle in his guts where it could do no harm. Soon he, Miranda, and the bed itself had become resonant, each with the other, thus preventing an essential element of successful woodling – the movement of one thing in opposition to another. And to further complicate this mystery Jim's head was filling with strains of *The more it snows, tiddely-pom*, an intermittent source of impotence since his adolescent years.

'Zat's eet, Zhim, keep my Aunty Zhane 'appy. Fill eet wiz your rooster. Do eet to me. Give eet to me 'ard.'

The more it goes, tiddely-pom . . .

She had quickly lost control and was tossing herself about like a dying fish.

'Miranda, I –'

'No words, Zhim. Zhust do eet.'

The more it goes, tiddely-pom, on snowing.

He shrugged. Her face had become a medically inadvisable shade of pink. As she jigged in each direction, her skin lagged behind its inner frame. She screamed and then – in a manner he'd remember for as long as he was allowed to live – she ripped her nails into his chest, fell forwards, and bit deeply into his shoulder. Jim jumped. Unhooking herself from him she quickly turned about face, splaying her thighs above his mouth and resting her chin on his thigh.

'I think ze time 'as come for anuzzer leetle snack.'

In the cream shadows of her, Jim was gritting his teeth.

iv

Oh well it is tedious me and Miriam we've had it upside down back to front her on top me down the bottom end with feathers cricket gloves Gales honey champagne champagne bottles condensed milk then Danish films starring huge black men with huge black personalities Miriam in silk Jim ditto on the stairs over the sewing machine under the kitchen table among fields so green they were toppling over in toilets at the British Museum some fine exhibits they have there sky-blue windows and April clouds as we wandered to Trafalgar Square *let's have a nice day in London* she'd said so there we were trying to establish our opinions on the power of those so-white buildings down in Whitehall where the real wheeler-dealers have set up shop we could hear their brains humming over what stunt to pull next the sky soft and harmless like that song by Aretha Franklin years ago making people sad for happiness till we came to our bench in the square and ate malt extract sandwiches you wouldn't waste money buying lunch from those daft shops so you'd brought it with you in a plastic bag the whole way on the train through fields of baby oil sunshine near Reading the Thames chopped and colourful as Monet would have presented it crowded with boats and you said you'd like to live *there* each time the train hurtled past one of those mock Tudor commuter houses occupied by chaps in fat shirts and kids playing soccer against the garage door and under rainbows thrown by fountains and the fixed stare of a sculpted lion we had our lunch throwing bits of crust to the pigeons and probably by then the sense had deepened of hating loving you or loving hating you the way you chewed the way you'd put our sandwiches in separate sides of the plastic carrier till on a bench just a crust's throw away a youngster turned up with her mum and dad no more than thirteen say and though she was wearing child's clothes viz an absurd damson hat, sequinned skirt and Jemima Puddleduck T-shirt there lay mystery in faintly swelling calves and the movements of her T-shirt and I was beginning to sense the tragedy of old Gustav von Aschenbach coming to love a Tadzio and the poor boy was representing something Gustav no longer owned and so it was with the girl on the bench swinging her legs chasing the pigeons always giggling yet warm lip legs with secrets here and there she'd bought seeds from a seedy-looking guy and was sprinkling them to the pigeons who flocked fluttered and fucked about her crimson shoes maybe you noticed Jim falling for her movements as he sat with greaseproof wrapping on his knees and mouthfuls of stoneground an ache caught up in dazzles of the white square the scent the prospect of landscapes in the National Gallery the splendour of ancient bells thanking Christ he didn't live there the thin slip bushy child woman incinerating his innards and when she bent down he snapped the damson of her loins or chicken shadows down her T-shirt over there another seedy guy holding out London tea-towels you could wipe up your plates with Buckingham Palace or poke Prince Charles down the insides of wine-glasses and in the corner of my eye Miriam chewing without opening her mouth using the same muscle at the hinge of her jaw that had spasms when she was on the warpath so maybe she'd spotted me turning to inks of the spirit over the damson girl and her seeds putting aside her own mystique with the zoo-man though marriage had required the gradual elimination of harmful substances from our diets turning them healthy healthy but as bland as jugged fish if there is such a thing and if there isn't there should be – jugged fish and low-everything margarine helping to prevent heart problems then bowels like autobahns through excess roughage not that you should have done the cooking in line with modern trends but you'd insisted to die to sleep curious things wives not wishing to go over the top about it but *something* happens to them we don't understand clutching at our parts as game wardens in the Ngoro-Goro crater may grasp serpents by the throat milking them of venom before harm can be done and in the midst of this a god never coming to explain things not even a hint the bugger just rumours of peace and rumours of aliens instead aliens all set to take over from Victor Kiam that evangelist of loot bristling onto the TV screens to tell us he'd become fucking loaded selling instruments to remove hair from places we didn't want it I was so impressed I bought the fucking company aren't I a fabulous bastard so the bum-hair remover's just round the corner it must come after ears bringing about a world of hairless capitalists some of whom were taking snapshots by the sculpted lion even now or even then I should say primeval Jim Jim the bastard Jim who should know better than to croon down innocent T-shirts Jim who longed for Spotty Dog with Spotty Dog things were OK Jim the hooligan of spiritual matters his face turned away from Miranda a speck in the eye of the Almighty if that and the girl in Trafalgar Square just before the world began to shrink buckling up I was trying to catch her eye but her mum and dad were keeping an eye on the chap with malt extract sandwiches his wife beside him in spasm around the jaw oh the girl in her hat throwing damson shadows her dad standing a few yards back to take a photo of her later we saw Tower Bridge Madame Tussauds the unmagnificence of Oxford Street yet the hat was on his mind in windows and through the narrow sky as Miriam bought waterbeds of the imagination and we were pushing against a tide of mankind coming up the pavement it had never occurred to me before that there were such things as French Chinamen but I heard them speaking as I waited for Miriam outside one of those famous stores damson hats bobbing among crowds on the far pavement and this cycle of wanting guffawed at by one generation after another though at least you feel you're telling the truth about some damn thing and those eyes the eyes of Judy Garland or the eyes of Laura watching seagulls through her opened window Jim the loathsome pirate scooping hatfuls of jewels to die to sleep Miranda sleeping her spine against his nose bold remarkable sunlight colouring the far wall hints of autumn her feet together her body sideways his arm slithering away from her inches at a time towards the edge of her bed whatever our histories may contain the result is always *this instant* don't y'know.

v

He dressed quietly in Miranda's bathroom, taking stock of soaps and razors, plastic hats, two bottles of Arabic hair conditioner – the presence of which comforted him somehow – a lump of pumice, stained-glass mobiles hanging above the toilet, a plastic Lech Walesa, a poster mounted under glass in an aluminium frame of a ginger cat wearing dark glasses. Primrose oil. In the kitchen he poured himself some orange juice, took a seat and looked out to the avenue, which was quiet with fallen lime leaves and one or two strollers who didn't seem to be paying heed to a shrinkage in pavement, carriageway, the houses themselves, nor to the widening blossom of sky. Across the road at the end of a short cul-de-sac he could see a conifer hedge broken by an ornate black gate. Through the gate from this angle he could just make out an ornamental garden and the corner of a building, toilets perhaps, or a pavilion of some kind.

Miranda's kitchen: her earthenware teapot, an unwashed glass vase full of coloured marbles, a magnetic frog on the fridge door holding a list of things to be done, a bowl of pears. The smallest drums sound warnings across human deserts. Jim was laughing into his hands. The trick lay in being able to imagine one's own retrospect. Through the glass front of the food cupboard he could see a cylinder of gravy granules, loose Oxo cubes arranged into a triangle, a packet of spaghetti, two sachets of dried soup and several half-sized tins of baked beans. On the cooker stood a saucepan with a metal lid thrown slightly off-centre by the intrusion of a wooden spoon. At the bottom of her list of things to be done, *The Tempest* had been circled in red felt-tip. From downstairs came the softened but determined movements of the guardians. Jim's eyes were sore with fatigue. Putting on his coat he crept into the hall to look in at Miranda, whose arm was hanging from the bed and who was breathing rhythmically with sleep. He went slowly down the stairs to the hall, then out of the front door.

The bus ride took fifteen minutes, carrying him back over the river, past the hospital and right through the centre of town. By the time he'd been deposited at the end of the crescent and walked the hundred yards home he'd reached the conclusion he was going mad, turning into a March hare, a curator of meaningless experiences, a jockey on the back of a single-minded horse. There should be limits to one's rebellion, even *in extremis*. As he crossed the weed-covered gravel parking-space he noticed that the varnish on the front door had cracked and was beginning to peel off. Holding his breath, he pressed his ear against the door, said a short prayer, then let himself in to the hall, gathering a few circulars from the mat and throwing them, as he always had, into a cardboard box left there for that purpose. Miriam enjoyed writing *Return to sender* on them and posting them back. He walked into the living room, listened again, then lay down on the sofa. The room was smaller than he remembered it. His favourite chair by the sideboard had been replaced by one similar but less threadbare, which used to be in Buggerface's room. Personal objects he liked to keep on a small table beside his chair had been cleared away, leaving just a circular piece of old lace and a garishly coloured vase. The smell was entirely Miriam. His larger mementoes were no longer lined along the mantelpiece, though the rack for Buggerface's old racing papers remained in the grate of the unused fireplace. It seemed Miriam had achieved the object of less clutter, the clutter having been made up previously of objects relating specifically to Jim. Worse still, the tiny white vase given to him by Laura one afternoon no longer stood in its sacred position. Perhaps Miriam had sniffed it out, though he couldn't remember ever having treated it with visible reverence. He linked his fingers, yawned and cracked his joints, unable to shake off a sense of no longer existing. The phone rang. He ignored it. Time flashed from the video recorder in brilliant green. The curtains had a freshness of colour, as though they'd recently been taken down and washed. He remembered the trouble he'd had fixing the rail, failing to drill deeply enough into the wall and breaking rawl-plugs by trying to force them home with a hammer. Miriam's slippers stood to attention by the side of the grate, the fur around their upper edges discoloured. Removal of his blockboard-mounted Stubbs had left a faint rectangle above the fireplace. Going into the kitchen, he put the kettle on and sat at the table. Autumn had the clarity of crystal as he looked at it through clean windows. She'd been up on a chair with a can of Sparkle. There were marigolds, snapdragons, a few late honeysuckle flowers. The leaves on the lilac were curling up, though he knew next year's buds would be waiting amongst them. The spirits refuse to bring time to a standstill. It all goes on and on. Nevertheless, the garden looked tired and even the latest shrubs lacked lustre and virility. By now a line of thicker cloud was climbing over the rooftops from the north-west. These were the shelves he had put up, and this the wallpaper he'd spent the weekend pasting. Tomorrow had been ringed in red on Miriam's wildlife calendar, though it was unlikely she too was going to *The Tempest*. As he unlocked and opened the kitchen door to air the room, a cat ran in and curled into a basket under the table. He was about to shoo it out when he realised it must live here. And on the notice-board hung a small photo of Christopher cut from *Zoo Illustrated*. Posing with a chimp this time. Unscrewing the lid from a ketchup bottle, Jim flicked a few spots at the bastard. From the day Miriam had started at the zoo nothing had been the same. Some air of vigour and contentment had enveloped her: a way of humming when putting on her make-up; skirts emphasising the firmness of her thighs; translucent blouses, damn it! We spot just about everything, we comrades of Beelzebub. And the tight one-piece woollen dress hugging every rise, each dip, a second skin. And as she stooped he'd seen daylight triangles of yesterday's dream. *Dear Miriam, Due to replacement of armchair and Christopher on noticeboard, am leaving you. Jim. PS. Hate cat.* As soon as the kettle had boiled, he made himself a coffee and drummed the table with his fingertips. Air from the garden was sweet and heavy, partially intoxicating him. The tree they'd planted on the occasion of moving in had turned a deep rust-red. And there was the rambling rose still climbing a trellis arched over the path; the damp tool-shed; the red-brick barbecue and the rustic seat made out of old logs where he'd sat on summer nights with the excuse of watching for owls or following the ascent of a silver moon. An over-romancing he'd allowed himself in softnesses of twilight. Watching Miriam at the living-room window, sipping from a glass of wine, the glass flashing in the light of a standard lamp. This the addictive mix of post-modern reflection. Since the walls are going, search yourself deep and down. Swim realms of motivation. Now he took the blue jug from the shelf and looked into it. Money, curled up and kept together with an elastic band. He counted it, taking thirty pounds on the basis this was his due by law. If the worst came to the worst Christopher would no doubt help her out. On the wall opposite still hung the large portrait – actually a photograph which, by some process, had been developed to look like an oil painting – of the whole of Miriam and Jim's immediate families sitting at a large refrectory table in a banqueting hall one dreary Lammastide Eve. A legion of twigs from the ancestral tree with grease from venison round plump chops. Chops as in mouth. Jim in the midst of it all, refusing to look at the camera, his sprouts untouched. Miriam opposite, a serviette in her left hand, the right one waving to the photographer, enjoying life. Buggerface this end in medieval wheelchair, allowed a large bowl of consommé. The rest of them raising their glasses, though Uncle Bob had also poked out his thumb and had put his head at an angle to indicate the cheeriness of human beings. *Sometimes I remember serenity and dog days in your arms.*

Throwing the rest of his coffee away, Jim went upstairs. Buggerface's room had gained a signed photo of Esther Rantzen but was otherwise the same – a spare zimmer frame tucked into the corner next to a plywood wardrobe, the old flower-painted chamber pot under the bed, his stainless steel spittle bowl, small plastic bottles containing night-time tablets, several tubes of ointment for bed-sores, a life-size black-and-white poster of Jeanette McDonald's head and, on the shelf next to the bed, the thesis. Jim opened it at random to find the chapter 'Underwear Without Tears', a favourite of his. He turned on the cylinder of oxygen kept as a precaution by the door and, pressing the mask to his face, took several deep breaths before crossing the landing to Miriam's room. The curtains had been opened wide and the upper half of the windows left open, making the air light and fragrant. His folding bed had been taken away. In its place stood a four-drawer tallboy he hadn't seen before. He sat at the side of the dressing table on an unstable padded chair he'd once rubbed down and varnished, then picked up one by one her knick-knacks, scraps of lace, a metal golly-brooch, various make-up things, with each a memory, a reference known only, perhaps, to Miriam and himself. Something new: a small leather-bound volume propped against a china candlestick, pages of coloured flower drawings. He could hear the arguments of sparrows bathing in the blocked guttering.

Fatigue tempted him to sprawl over Miriam's bed. On the cabinet beside him lay a tray with two unwashed cups and a plate covered in toast crumbs. He was facing the wall, tucking his hands between his knees for a think. Could detect her in the pillows as if he hadn't been absent, this smell of her a symbol of old recognition between familiars in the dark. Her boudoir, softened by drapes, an embroidered eiderdown, heavily varnished furniture, an old stuffed owl beneath a glass dome, the autumnal colours of long ago all langorous with perfumes of daytime, her skin, aromatic oils, bowls of pot pourri. Dangerous to lie horizontal. He pulled himself up, lighting a cigarette and taking out the *The Blue Kiosk*. After one pull on the cigarette he changed his mind and stubbed it out against the toast-plate, the faint noises outside joining sounds of memory or imagination – Miriam singing at the seaside in her flesh bikini or walking towards hems of surf as if she'd been practising with a book on her head, her feet splaying slightly and landing heel first, the thigh-flesh tightening, loosening, and the rush all around of sea against smooth rocks, how some of this power, awfulness, could become a bonding in itself; then moments of jealousy as other men watched her pass, a mixture of peace, sunlight, blue lagoons. He was running to catch her up, as on all holidays, running to catch her up. Watching the dream of her hand in Christopher's gives him the collywobbles, whereas a review of those automobile days with Laura pleasure him to death, sure of his reasoning, not Miriam's.

If you come back with Christopher I'll give him a radical vasectomy with my craft knife. Miriam, you had the coolest legs in town, slinking meaty in rumours of nylon warmth on church-bell mornings brown through pealing streets, and each time I came up the stairs with your coffee it was as if I'd dreamed up someone called Miriam overnight who, at dawn, proved to be nothing like you. Buggerface hadn't died in the night, and as you twisted up and round to drink it the low neckline of your nightgown pulled against your breast, the skin overnight brown, freckled in summer, tracing them in games, taking in some old smell of you, nipples vague bullseyes, you were hooking your legs out of bed and yawning rather than risking attentions at that time of day, and anyway Buggerface was due to go on a Fun Day with the Zimmer club, needed his tub of gruel and flask of rum-laced horlicks. They'll sub-title this life *A Carousel of Almosts*.

His arms, legs and abdomen had fallen further into dozing than his head. From next door came a smell of cats, meat-juices, and there was an emptiness in his throat as if he might have been hungry, though the moment passed. This was almost suspended animation but for the now-and-then sounds from the road making him jump, the clatter of a gate, someone whistling, a car horn, the rattle of garden tools in a wheelbarrow. She'd been here in moonlight applying creams, pulling on a thin nightgown and thumping towards him. He'd been trying to lie naked without shame. Smelling, she was, of bluebells, woodsmoke, stars of royal beauty bright, hot chestnuts, evensong, and this town was so quiet he wanted to roar above the rooftops, things like that going through his mind even as those impotent liquids poured into her.

vi

I can still see in my mind's eye the drawing Oswald brought to divinity classes; a skilful Ark of the Covenant crayoned in yellow to represent gold, for which he received the obligatory ten out of bloody ten. He smirked right through break. The teacher began calling him Oswald whenever she came across him in the corridor. He would describe other artistic projects in which he was currently involved, wish her good afternoon, then walk on ahead of me, hands playing in his pockets. My own picture – of Israelites – brought no such accolade and I have reached the conclusion this was because my heart wasn't in them. The Israelites, I mean. It's hard for unworldly boys to bring accuracy to the clothing and skin colour of overseas races, however downtrodden they may be. I think you need to be an Israelite yourself if you want to show conviction in your representations of them. And this outlook has remained through the Cold War, Cod War, Vietnam, the three-day week, episodes of Crossroads, and all manner of Middle-Eastern machinations; though whereas the Israelite outfits were once simple cloaks and scraps of rag they now look very well turned out as they duck to the roar of jets and those previously barren sands self-seed with timeshare apartments for which couples named Frank and Agatha from Rochdale have already signed and paid. It doesn't take a great deal of imagination to realise that if Jesus came back today there would hardly be anyone he liked much, Israelites or not, though I think he'd quite enjoy meeting Oswald if only for the thrill of having done so.

I won't forget our Latin lessons, the desks we sat at scratched with the obscenities of others as we half-looked through the windows at sugar girls leaping hurdles or hugging one another on those blue afternoons.

Oswald's days were asphyxiated with love, first for one, then another, and though the years between are now clouded, our walks home from school are clear as tumblers of iced lemonade: his face ashen, hopeful, mostly nose, as we stamped alongside the hawthorn hedge. Beyond it was a field whose cycles we followed week by week: watched as it was ploughed and planted; how it grew green and tall, then fine and yellow till, while we were away for the summer, it was harvested, the stubble burnt; and we'd return to watch the ploughing take place again one Autumn afternoon, a surf of seagulls outcackling the tractor. Oswald would pick up leaves to put between the pages of thick books. Years later the leaves probably slipped out when he least expected them reminding him that – say what you like about yesterday – it could be colourful still.

At a dip in the road by the old mill one day we leaned over the fence to watch minnows and bullheads in the stream below and it was there a miracle took place. We were joined by Samantha whose stature, long hair and dream-laden eyes are with me still. Excellent at badminton, rich, aristocratic in posture – how she came to talk to Oswald, heaven only knows. He had a cold, as I recall, never the best of experiences for his close companions. And we'd heard rumours that Samantha's younger twin sisters – Marigold and Bethany – were beautiful too. Samantha pushed between us to see what this fuss was over fishes and, while doing so, invited us to her house the following weekend. I remember a certain rubbing of hands and bouncing up and down on Oswald's part. She drifted away from us, her skirt being tossed from side to side, overthrowing any dreams he still entertained over Laurinda and Jane, both of whom had become moody and apt to rages he didn't understand.

Samantha's father was an Israelite himself, though of the modern kind in exile, owning a mansion which stood at the edge of a crescent lawn strewn with century-old cedars of Lebanon and – at that time of year – garden furniture, golden retrievers and badminton nets. The mansion itself boasted flagstone corridors, stags' heads, crossed axes and an original oil of Prince Albert showing what a cheeky-looking fellow with sideburns he used to be. It was Oswald's opinion that Prince Albert had the worst of a bad deal: wife like a lump of anthracite and nothing much to pass the time. Samantha showed us all round, then took us on to the lawn where Oswald happily surveyed the acres of cedars, rhododendrons and daughters spread before him. He was spoilt for choice and I suspect that had time allowed he would have drawn up a roster. God was once more in mortal danger. After all, each daughter *deserved* it. Each exceeded Oswald's previous expectations and each was as beautiful as a windless summer evening, their features angular and sleek, their bodies – later described by him as 'awakened' – slim and apparently quite without bones or inconveniences of that kind. Also invited was a friend of theirs with no such sophistication, a heavy-footed tom-girl who had summed up Oswald on her arrival and refused to modify her opinion.

Previously the nearest we'd come to salmon was a dark paste scooped on knives from ribbed jars, but here at a table on the lawn lay pink chunks of it in oriental bowls. Oswald was in his long Mass-trousers and Padawaxed shoes, a napkin hanging from the collar of his white shirt like a steamed Dover sole. The heavens rang with meadowlarks, hummed with acrobatic bi-planes made musical by those words of tissue which occasionally drifted from a daughter's pale lips. The twins were dark-haired with Israelite noses and skin the colour of elephant tusks, while Samantha, a head taller than both of them, lay against the landscape like the weakest most beautiful breath of cornwind. Her father ruminated over a salmon sandwich, his bald head glowing in the sunshine, pretending to talk of mathematics but actually experimenting with Oswald to gauge the effect such bringing-out of daughters would have on him and his labouring friend. And will he have caught the excitement in Oswald's eyes at that first taste of Earl Grey after so many years of Co-op 99?

It soon became clear that someone had instructed these girls how to eat a sandwich without once being seen to open their mouths, chew or swallow, bringing Oswald to a state of unspoken panic that someone might notice the pâté of bread and salmon touring his gums like smalls in a washing-machine. The tom-girl had been placed at the far end out of harm's way – to avoid, perhaps, unintentional comparison – and though Oswald may not have realised, it was she – with her quiet lack of sophistication, honesty and look of faint amusement – who outshone the others.

Oswald's discomfort continued till Mr Israelite excused himself, leaving us to finish tea and have a game of badminton. The court was bathed in mauve shadows falling from the cedar trees. The tom-girl sat it out on the verandah steps. The three daughters in turn moved about the badminton court, floating into the air with raised racquets to return soft shuttlecocks, their hair cascading above them as they floated back to earth in dresses of translucent cloud. Oswald, bless him, tumbled around like a new-born foal, snorting whenever a humour of the situation got the better of him, and his most glamorous shot resulted in racquet rather than shuttlecock crossing the net. By that time Samantha had retired to a Lloyd loom chair to study the poetry of William Blake and break hearts. Her tom-girl friend had extended an arm and was rubbing a sun-cream into it. Then there was the imagination of a finger – and nothing more – reaching for the top of her blue jeans as we sat cross-legged upstairs in the twins' room playing tracks from Woodstock and talking of the ascent of mankind, both of which Oswald had missed. Samantha went on to emphasise the part the Israelites had played in the latter, while the tom-girl lay back trying to balance a riding-crop on her nose. Joe Cocker, wet and slightly crazy, was asking *What would you do if I sang out of tune?* By that time I was at the window watching a certain ballet of light among the cedars, the swing of one colour with another, green mostly, quiet lime to most seductive jade.

The whole episode had taken four to five hours. We were ejected by the father because it was time for the girls' baths and their hour's study. They waved to us and the tom-girl as we crossed the lawn. We waved back. The tom-girl wouldn't come any further with us, choosing instead a shaded pathway through the woods. Having shaken Oswald's hand she shook his spirit by kissing my cheek and leaving upon it a perfume of bluebells and woodsmoke. A stranger who had said hardly two words all afternoon.

It wasn't till she was out of sight that Oswald began his poor impression of Fred Astaire. He didn't care a jot about the tom-girl's kiss anyway. Something about Samantha's behaviour had made him suspect she had a thing for him. Perhaps it had been her way of ignoring most everything he did or said, her refusal to be his partner in the badminton doubles, or the teaspoon of trifle she'd flicked at him as he made his way to the toilet – which he'd called the bathroom. Coming back he'd obviously been thinking his life through because he was wanting to know if any of us knew the surname of the guy who'd had a hit with 'Maria'. Malcolm something. We were still thinking of it as we walked home. Malcolm *something*. An out-of-reality singer with Shredded Wheat hair which would unravel itself the moment he tried real things like changing a wheel on Maria's car.

Anyway, that was the lyric, with slight adaption, Oswald sent Samantha first thing Monday morning.

vii

First of all the sound of car doors slamming and an interweaving of voices – one low, one high – mere side-shows to an imagination Jim was having, but when a scuffle of voices came up the path and a key slid into the front door he gathered up his cigarettes, lighter and *The Blue Kiosk*, carefully put them in his carrier bag, climbed off the bed and then, seeing no alternative, shuffled under it to a realm of old shoes, unused bedding and empty luggage, cushioning his head on a soft holdall which had been lying in the far corner. In the hall Miriam gradually stopped crying and suggested the other person leave her now, she'd be all right, thank you. The second voice, a smooth, zoo baritone, wouldn't hear of it. His place was with her. Miriam's reasoning was that if he continued to skive just because she was having a few days off, the bosses would soon reach conclusions; whereupon the deeper voice said: 'Let them reach them then.' This Jim found grammatically unsatisfying. There was movement away from the hall, doors opening, an exclamation from Miriam that someone had been lying on her sofa, then the deeper voice from the kitchen saying, 'And someone's been drinking your coffee.' Whereupon Miriam hurried to join the deeper voice. A set of keys were dropped on to the washing machine, a fuss of the cat was made by the man, and it was Miriam, presumably, who pressed the switch on the kettle. And here were Jim's old trainers, kept secret at the far side of the bed to remind him of wading cold, pebbled waters. Just a quid, in a sale of bankrupt stock. Miriam hadn't wanted to be seen in the company of a man who'd wear a combination of yellow swimwear and crimson-sided trainers, and quite right too in her breast-coloured costume; but at least he'd avoided cutting his feet or being stung by jellyfish while she, legs wide in league with sun-lovers, rubbed and shook her thighs with tanning cream, light catching the grease of it at the leg-lines of her costume, fingers frequently slipping beneath its elastic.

Christopher: 'Well there's nothing you can do about it . . . *mumble cough*.' Followed by the onset of hysteria, stage one, from Miriam, which soon became laughter of the kind reserved for people who are not Jim – a touch of the cocktail party about it, calculated amusement over *petit-fours*, chuckles with salted peanuts and lashings of Pomagne. Incoherence and gentleness then; and small talk, lovers' talk over zoo-things – the mood swings of anteaters, those bastard tramps rustling Angoras to make stews behind the bus station. Miriam's heels toured the living room again, then thumped through into the bathroom while Christopher prepared drinks and hummed a zoo-song, maybe something from *Doctor Doolittle*. 'Hey Miri! Come and . . . *mumble mumble*.' The toilet-roll holder rattled. The flush was pulled, Miriam marched back through the hall and living room but stopped before she reached the hard kitchen floor. A yell of harassment and indignation. Most probably they'd spotted money missing from the blue jug. Then *tap tap tap*, Miriam tapping across the kitchen, perhaps into Christopher's arms for a conciliatory hug. She'd see, round the edge of his neck, flecks of ketchup over the journal cutting. Jim could be so resentful when he had a mind.

For ten minutes he couldn't hear a word and took the opportunity to move a little further towards the wall, spitting breath to keep disturbed fibres and tumbleweeds of fluff from his nose and eyes. Downstairs, chairs were eventually pushed away, cups swilled under the tap and left to dry on the draining-board. Jim snapped his breathing as both pairs of feet came up the stairs and pushed their way into the bedroom.

'Oh, for God's sake, look. He's been lying on my bed.'

Jim could see Christopher's shoes directly behind Miriam's. The zoo-man was ready to give a protective embrace which might develop, might not. He wasn't going to make a big thing out of it. Not every woman wanted to make love when their sanctuary had so recently been penetrated. Coming to the bedside, she straightened the covers, sat down and cried once more.

'Why did he have to do this now? Why?'

Christopher's shoes crossed the room and settled beside hers. 'Don't be daft. He's obviously in a state. Wouldn't you be?'

'Mr Cook said he'd taken it with no trouble at all. In fact he said he'd seemed quite relieved.'

'Yes, but that's often how it goes, isn't it? I don't expect the shock hit him till later. Now he's gone barmy.'

'He should have stayed here then. At least till I got back. Why didn't he tell me what was happening?'

'Perhaps he's on his way to the hospital thinking that's where you'll be.'

'In that case, he wouldn't have taken the money, would he? He knows how much I need it.'

Their weight had pushed the spring base to within inches of Jim's nose.

'Come on love. Don't upset yourself. What's thirty quid?'

'Do you think I'd better ring the hospital?'

'Don't see the point. They know he's done a runner. If he goes back, fine. If he doesn't, there's not a lot they can do about it. He'll show up. Leave it for now.'

'We had one of our arguments yesterday.'

'Miri. You've got to understand how people are in that situation. He must be very edgy. Up one minute, down the next. Don't start blaming yourself. He's not to be relied on at the moment. He'll see sense later and do the right thing.'

Despite Jim's keener perception of human nature it was still with some surprise that he watched both pairs of feet lift gradually out of view behind the valance and an area of the bed towards the back wall bulge downwards. He had been gathering fluff which he compressed in his fist. Complaints from the springs and much movement suggested that the pair were lying side by side.

'What time's old Tobias coming back?'

'Not for another two hours.'

'Mmmm. Good.'

'What do you mean, good?'

'Huh! What do I mean? she says.'

'Oh don't start. I'm not in the mood.'

'You were last night.'

'I told you, that was just an exception. I don't really want you here. It's too risky.'

'No offence but your uncle wouldn't notice if we had sex swinging from his zimmer frame.'

'And what if Jim comes back?'

'Why should he come back? He's been here and gone away. And whatever his plans are, now he's seen two cups on the tray here I don't expect he's very pleased with you at the present.'

'Oh don't say that. I knew I shouldn't have left them there. I was late. And it was all your fault. You're so selfish sometimes.'

'Come on. You know you were having fun. You didn't mind the thought of being late then, did you?'

'That was ages ago. Before all this.'

'You can't fool me. There's a shine in your eyes even now.'

'Don't you ever think of anything else?'

'Not where you're concerned.'

'I don't believe this. Serve you right if you get the sack.'

Though Jim was nodding, Christopher's spirit continued to rise. 'Fuck the zoo.'

'And leave my blouse alone. Why can't you have a bit of respect. A bit of finesse. It cost as fortune.'

'I love unwrapping you, Miri.'

'Oh for goodness sake go away.'

'Shan't.'

A sound as of a sea-lion coming round from a general anaesthetic. The bed undulating in various quarters. Soft protests. Items of clothing falling to the floor. Eventually Miriam's naked feet slipped into view. Crooked, crusted, yellow-bottomed feet. Jim hadn't noticed them so clearly before. Not objectively. Small – how could he put it? – small, *snubbed* feet. They walked to the window. She was drawing the curtains. Suddenly she stopped and said 'If only I knew for sure what he was doing.' It crossed his mind to swing round, poke out his arm and take hold of her ankle, but he stayed still, arms by his sides, his fists clenched.

Christopher yawned. 'I love it when you stand on tiptoe.'

She half laughed in response. Her feet came back to the bed and slid upwards. The springs sank. Jim was crossing his ankles and bringing his arms up to form a cross on his chest, trying to relax by way of a serenity technique Laura had once taught him whereby you ordered each piece of yourself to become calm, starting with the toes. It began well but by the time he'd reached his knees the toes had relapsed. For some minutes the fingers on his right hand had been tingling. His liver ached and a dull throbbing had begun in the small of his back. And there was an awkward moment when he had to hold his breath to stave off a cough.

'You've a wonderful mouth, Miri. I love licking the corner of it. Like this.'

'Don't. Don't. Not now. You know what happens to me. I could kill you sometimes.'

'You can't fool me you've taken your clothes off by accident. God oh God, I wish I had more hands to touch you all at once.'

'Supposing he's just gone to get something from the shop?'

'Oh come on Miri. Be fair. Let go for Christ's sake.'

'If he came back now I'd die.'

'Don't make me feel any worse. I haven't got anything against the poor bugger but there's nothing we can do this minute, is there? He's old enough to make his own decisions. And there's no sense spoiling things just because he's . . . not well.'

'It's tearing me apart. Surely you understand.'

'I *do* understand, but I thought we had an agreement not to talk about him at inappropriate times.'

'Uoph! Don't do that. God you're like a bull at a gate sometimes.'

'Sorry.'

'It's knowing he's been here. I mean, what must he be thinking? He deserves some peace of mind at least.'

'Don't do this to yourself, love. We've been having this relationship and I don't see any reason why that should change just because of . . . No sense crucifying yourself. You feel things. Of course you do. You're bound to, but –'

'I'm still married to him.'

'Oh, here we go. Bring on the violins. Listen. Can I just say two little words? *Not now*. Not now for heaven's sake. For my sake. We've been through all this a hundred times.' The sound of lips and springs as someone changed position. 'How about one of my massages, hey? You need calming down. Look, put your arms like that. No, lie back. You're neck's rigid. Fine, now open your legs a bit. Further. Hang on, if I just kneel between them. Oooph. There. Hold the headboard. I said hold the headboard. Now, close your eyes. Don't do a thing, just listen to the sound of my voice, let yourself drift. Imagine you're on an island with . . . with white warm sand, a brilliant blue sea, a bottle of vodka. I'm a tanned islander who can't speak a word of English. We're in the shade of a coconut tree. There we are. Listen to the lapping waves, the call of seabirds, the laughter of black women watching from a rock – yeah, you like that don't you? My fingers and lips are breezes tickling your skin. Here they brush your neck, your shoulders, breasts, belly-button, your succulent waist, your skin glistening with Ambre Solaire. Hey, can I use some of this hand cream again?'

'Mnnn.'

A dribble was propelled from the almost empty bottle with a sound as of someone using a straw to suck up the last drops of a milkshake. Miriam took a deep breath. Jim also.

'Mnnnnn.'

'That's it, relax. Drift away. Feel those breezes here and here and here. No, keep them closed. Remember the sea and the cooing of those black girls. Maybe it's too much for them and they're gently unhooking one another's saris. Here's the wind brushing your thigh, your mound of venus, the very secrets of your inner thighs . . . '

'Saris are Hindu things.'

'Does it fucking matter? Keep still.'

'Can I let go of the headboard yet?'

'No you can't. Wait. That's the secret of everything. Wait.'

'Not there. Oh.'

Jim was stifling a yawn and rotating his shoulders to ease his back.

'No, please. Stay where you are. For once I want you to have all your pleasures first. Now, as I lift your knees I want you to dream of those black girls, splay your legs as wide as you can and talk to me.'

'What about?'

'Don't be dim. You know.'

'But Christopher . . . '

'Hold the bloody headboard I said.'

Miriam's breathing deepened. A movement in the springs seemed to indicate she was digging her heels into the bed. By this time Christopher's foot was resting on the floor. There was an elastoplast round its second toe which had obviously been in place for several days. Pressure exerted on the foot was turning the other toes white. A sound of wet fish. Regular movement.

'And these are dark fingers walking slowly down your thigh. You wish to protest but you're too tired. Too exhilarated. Talk to me for God's sake.'

'You know I'm no good at that sort of thing.'

'And soon, when you least expect it, you will feel those graceful fingers playing among the tendons and muscles here, just here. The sound of the sea rises to a roar. The wind gathers and begins to tug at the palm fronds. You're not sure whether to scream or die. It's all too much. Desperate hands are tying your wrists to the tree while others pull your ankles apart and waves crash to the shore and as you open your eyes you see a beautiful, beautiful mouth reaching for your . . . *Ahhhh*, oh no!'

'Bloody hell! Mind where you're . . . '

'Sorry, sorry. It just happened.'

Miriam sighed. 'Doesn't matter. Just hand me one of those tissues, quick.'

'I was sure it was going to be all right this time.'

'Don't keep on. I understand. You get yourself too worked up. *Tissue*.'

Christopher's foot slid out of sight. 'Here.'

'More than that. Give me a handful. Look!'

'Sorry.'

'Watch out. There's a bit on the pillow.'

After a while a clump of sculpted tissue fell into Christopher's left shoe. Jim watched it for a long time. Pain had formed a wide, tight band round his waist. He wanted a cigarette and, having decided a taste was better than nothing, carefully opened the packet in his plastic bag, manipulated a cigarette between his lips, and sucked.

'Maybe we should have a rest and try again in a minute.'

'There isn't time for God's sake. I have to do some shopping before Tobias gets back. There's nothing for his tea. Nothing runny enough, anyway.'

'Don't say that. I wanted to please you. I feel terrible now.'

'We shouldn't be doing this anyway. I told you we shouldn't during the day, when he's due home.'

'Yeah, you're right. Poor old bugger. Still, if he wasn't around we'd have more chance, wouldn't we? Can't help thinking about it sometimes.'

'Don't start. You know how I feel about that.'

'These Council homes are great nowadays. The old folk are warm and well cared for and there's always someone around in an emergency.'

'He's a bit of a burden but I'm not sentencing him to a plastic chair for the rest of his life.'

'Sometimes you have to think of yourself.'

'I'm not like that . . . Ow! Don't do that. You've finished now.'

'I can't help it. I want to make it up to you. One of those things you always said about Jim was that you weren't satisfied. I keep worrying you'll get fed up if it goes wrong with me too.'

'No sense fishing when you've run out of . . . Huh! Would you credit it? There's another dollop there. Look. On the table leg.'

'You're not very romantic are you? Sometimes I think you don't like the essential me.'

'We haven't got time for the essential-you argument.'

'You know. *Like* me. Really like me. *Me*. And sometimes you're so hostile. *Bitter* and hostile.'

'Please Christopher. Let's –'

'It's just an observation. How far have we really come if I can't make a simple observation? I do my best to make you . . . well, satisfied, but it's like I'm an instrument of yours. Not all the time. Just now and again.'

'We've had quite a day of it and I don't want one of

those arguments. Especially with Tobias coming home.'

'You're not being very fair. I mean, I only want to talk.' The bed moved as if Christopher was sitting up.

'But this is how it starts. You're in a state because of what happened just now. And you always blame me in the end. You're the hostile one.'

'Knew it! Knew it! You're pissed off about my difficulty.'

'No Christopher. You've got it all wrong.'

'Well hard luck. I've said what I've said and I'm sticking to it. There's nothing wrong with me at all. It's you, and I won't be told otherwise. And if you're going to be like this you can pissing well piss off. I've taken three days leave because of you and now you're just being a bag.'

'You didn't tell me you were on leave!'

'I wanted to make you happy. Obviously I shouldn't have bothered.'

'Listen, you can hardly blame me for not being pleased over something I didn't know about.'

Was that a palm being slapped to a forehead? Jim's filter tip had become soft and tasteless. He turned the cigarette round and was about to take his first suck when something struck the wall at the far end of the room.

'That cup was brand new!'

'Fuck your cup.'

'Oh well. For all the good you've done me I might as well.'

'Told you. See, I told you that was at the heart of it.'

'Don't talk rubbish.'

'Rubbish? It's not rubbish at all. You're the one in a

mood. Me? I'm calm as anything. And if you don't zip your lip I'll break the other fucker.'

'Go ahead. If you can't ejaculate at the right time, become destructive. That's what you men usually do.'

A second crash. Christopher cleared his throat. 'There we are. Shall I do the plate or do you want to take over?'

'I don't need to express myself like that.'

'Oh. Well I do now. You've driven me to it, haven't you? I may be throwing the plate but you're the force behind it, if the truth were known.'

A third.

'I hope you'll be clearing it all up.'

'Fat chance of that, my dear. You can piss off.'

'Since this is my house I think you're the one who should leave. And don't keep using those foul words. They don't suit you.'

'Aha!'

'What now?'

'I knew it. I *knew* it. You've contrived this whole thing to get me out of the way. Just as I bloody thought. Poor old Jim does something unexpected and you go to pieces. I've noticed you know. I notice *everything*. You don't mind him dying as long as it's on your terms. And you don't give a damn about me. You want a way to end it without having to blame yourself afterwards. *Let's get Christopher mad* you're thinking. Well, congratufuckinglations, it's worked. I'm going to put on my clothes, then I'm getting out of here and you won't see me for dust.'

'Do what you like. I'm not going to be emotionally blackmailed.'

'Blackmailed?' the bedside lamp fell to the floor.

'Blackmailed? You're the one who's fond of that little game.'

His feet thumped to the floor. A pair of hands reached down to gather a pair of maroon Y-fronts.

'If you could only come at the right time you wouldn't be like this now. And you know you'll regret it if you storm out. You haven't the guts to go, really. Don't you remember how you were last week? Ended up creeping back in with presents practically begging for mercy?'

'That was then. This is now.'

He collected his socks. His shirt and trousers jerked upwards. He sat on the bed, feet thrust within spitting distance of Jim. The socks were put on. He grunted as he lifted the wet tissue from his shoe. Lying to one side were Miriam's stockings.

'I bet you won't get more than a hundred yards . Why don't you just stop it? Why?'

'Listen. There's not a hope in hell I'm going to regret anything.' His voice was low, though its edges were like a fine saw. When he had finished tying his laces, he walked forwards, then turned to face the bed. 'Right, Mrs Misery Chops, I'm going then. And for the record I want you to know I don't give a toss for your cups or the plate. And I won't be back here. Not in a million years.'

Jim could almost hear the expression on Christopher's face. He saw the shoes shuffle close to the bed. Heard a kiss.

'See you soon,' she said.

'Don't bet on it sweetheart. But I'll ring you when you've had a chance to see how fucking mad you've been.' Turning, he stalked out of the room. His shoes moved with a certain deliberation and confidence for the first eleven stairs, but he stumbled at the bottom and swore. The front door slammed. Jim thought he heard Miriam laugh. She swung off the bed and went downstairs to wash. He took the opportunity to make himself more comfortable. A short while later she came back to the bedroom. A small hand gathered up her thin underclothes. He listened as they were hitched, hung and hushed around her body, her smell deepening like mock orange on a warm evening. She used the bed as a seat while pulling on her stockings. He watched each foot lift in turn and carefully breathed in deep to catch the memory of her. When she had finished dressing she straightened the bed and replaced the lamp, then started to collect the broken china; but soon she dropped the pieces, swore softly to herself and left the room. A few minutes later she was thumping down the path. The gate clattered. Her Honda took a while to start but eventually pulled off. He listened till its hum had died away.

It was raining. He rolled out of his hiding place, lit a cigarette and stretched himself. On his way out of the bedroom he opened each drawer of the chest, pushing his hands over her jumpers, squeezing the lumps of tucked-together socks, splaying his fingers among the softness of her underwear, over the plastic fronts of unopened stocking packets, the delicate cottons of her camisoles. Pressed her bedsocks and vests to his mouth. The rain was composing cool melodies over roofs, roads and trees. He found his old waxed coat folded at the bottom of the wardrobe and put it on over his jacket. For a time he walked back and forth between the living room and kitchen, but then left the house, heading in the direction he knew he wouldn't come across her if she returned. On his way out of the crescent, he counted a dozen inquisitive faces hanging from neighbouring windows.

viii

He walked slowly, counting paces from one lamp-post to the next, thirty, sometimes twenty-nine, on the road to Innisfree, pavements cracking widthways, rain running from the underside of privets. Beneath the Post Office awning stood a bouquet of elderly ladies, some with husbands grouching at truants through pipefuls of Navy Cut. And what has distracted us but dreams of a plot of land inspired by the diaries of Edith Holden (of which they unearthed another volume – how fortunate). The men wore macs of metallic blue, while elderly wives had transparent plastic waterproofs and transparent plastic hats. Glimpses of those tight, plump uniforms beneath. Splashes of geranium and cenotaph grey. Old folk queuing in the rain, around them regiments of houses standing to attention this way and that, their lines broken by a church, the jumble-sale hall. Days here and there had been similar, wet with no composition, and there was no attitude to take other than compliance when the town lay still as fact at your feet, scurried through by Georges and Berthas – not that you'd condemn then in any way because they were sweet old souls, but there was always the suspicion you could take a George or a Bertha from over there and replace them with one of *these* and cause but scant inconvenience. It would often seem on those wet days that a new companion scratched would reveal an incipient George or Bertha hankering for sensible shoes and loose woollen cardies.

Then your uncertainties could fill cool moonlights.

The bus shelter had been hastily built a few yards from a white-painted bridge which carried the road over a rock-filled stream and a meadowed glen lined with willows. Jim had seen the nineteenth-century paintings of the glen coloured green and gold with stags drinking in the still of twilight, but the plaque beside the paintings had been careful to explain that this had been a somewhat romantic view of things. Along the stream these days a number of sculptures commissioned by the Arts Council looked out at you if you walked by: slim men with bald heads and no suggestion of genitalia; abstract lions; an eagle with human arms in place of wings.

The shelter was a grey cube with a wooden seat along its back wall and a wire-mesh rubbish bin in one corner. Though he ducked as he passed through its entrance, the lintel still scraped the back of his waxed jacket. He took from his pocket a clump of tissue and wiped the seat, which had become damp with rain being blown through the observation hole. Pieces of tissue broke off to form wet lumps which he brushed away before sitting down. And though he pushed himself right back his knees were still tight against the front wall and if he raised himself more than an inch or so his hair would flatten against the ceiling. Gripping the edge of the seat, he looked out. His journey had been too slow and there had been times when he'd been tempted to turn back. Now he counted heavy drops of rain which were falling from the tree-canopy and splashing against the roof. He'd noticed the pinched whiteness of his fingertips as he fumbled for a cigarette. A passing car ripped water from the road surface. He couldn't decide what number bus to take, which destination to name, or how much fare he should pay. He'd been keeping his eye on a splash of black in the distance which seemed to be running, though it hadn't come much closer: someone in a raincoat with head bowed under a black hood smacking crimson shoes to the pavement. Love was like sand revealed by the tide on which you stamped your footprints for a while till the tide returned. Yes, it was a girl moving towards him, though the time she was taking bore no relation to the distance involved. As he turned away, a sudden gust of wind brought her flapping through the entrance and for a moment her breathless figure stole most of the daylight from him. There was so little space widthways she couldn't help tucking against him as she threw off her hood and sat down.

'I thought I would drown,' she said.

Fixing his attention on the rubbish bin, Jim nodded. He could see from the corner of his eye that she was examining the side of his face, her head tilted slightly. 'Is it me or has this shelter got smaller? I can't remember having to squeeze up like this.'

Jim moistened his lips. 'I think you're right,' he said.

'I used to be able to put my legs out but now there's hardly room to sit at all.'

'Don't worry. It's not you. You're quite all right.'

'Good,' she said. 'That's a relief.'

Jim turned to the observation hole. A large dark cloud had brought with it a more vigorous wind which had turned the shower into a squall. 'It's not just the bus shelter either,' he said.

She laughed. 'No. I've noticed it all over the place. I've been keeping a record.'

'Good for you.'

Jim risked one look at her. She had unbuttoned her coat to reveal a red blazer, grey jumper and black pleated skirt. Her legs looked the whiter in contrast to it all. 'You're late home from school.'

'I had two free periods so I hopped it for the afternoon. I've been walking around. Then this rain started.'

He was beginning to suspect he'd seen her before and was trying to establish the context, but – for the moment – it wouldn't come.

She had pushed her hands against the roof of the shelter. 'And where are you going then?'

He smiled. 'I don't know. I haven't decided.'

'Well,' she said, letting her hands fall to her lap, 'you'd better make up your mind, hadn't you? There's that sign which says "Tender exact fare and state destination." I like the word tender, don't you? On buses and trains they never ask you to hand over your money. You have to tender it.'

Jim was shaking his head. 'And what about you? Where are you going?'

'Home I suppose.'

'And how much does it cost to get there?'

'Fifty-five pence. Why?'

'So, if I said, say, seventy-five, that would cover me for all eventualities.'

'I'm not sure they do a seventy-five. I don't think the town's that wide. But you can try.'

She stood up, buckling at the knees and pushing at the roof as if to heave it off. Then, wandering outside, she scuffed the pavement and gazed up and down the road before twisting on the heels of her crimson shoes, ducking back through the entrance and flopping down.

175

'Have you ever wondered what it would be like if we sat in here for ever and the bus didn't come and then everyone else, all the cars and things, faded away? Ever thought of that?'

Jim nodded. His chill had brought a slight soreness to the back of his throat.

'I'd be dead scared,' she said. 'I always think of that when it's raining. This is a really weird place you know.'

Jim was uncomfortable with his knees against the wall, but wouldn't twist to face her. In the meantime it had occurred to him where he'd seen her before and he was comforted by the miracle of it. And what makes them miracles is that they are never the outcomes you would have planned. They surprise and reassure you, bring about a certain peace and reverence.

'I don't think you should be talking to me, should you? I'm what you will have heard referred to as a stranger.'

She thumped him on the shoulder. 'Don't be silly. Anyway, you're not a stranger. I remember seeing you before. But then that's not surprising in a place this tiddly.'

'I don't think it was here. I'm sure it wasn't.'

Over the last few minutes he had noticed an *absence*, and it was only after careful consideration of the matter that he realised it had something to do with birdsong, or rather a lack of birdsong, and with a sudden dying of the wind and an easing of the rain. The glen, the road, the town itself, had become uncomfortably quiet. Twisting round, the girl squeezed herself against the side wall and struggled to lift her feet onto the bench. With her arms pulling hard against her shins she eventually managed it. Her shoes dug into his thigh. She folded her arms across her knees and rested her chin against them. Her legs were shaking.

'You look like death warmed up.'

'I've been having a difficult time of it.'

She made a click of displeasure with her tongue. 'Why is it you older people have so many bad days? It's the same with my mum and dad. They're always fighting something you can't put your finger on and it's only when they manage to beat it that they have a *good* day. My dad reckons being alive's bloody uncomfortable most of the time. That's what he says, anyway.'

In what he hoped was an avuncular fashion, Jim jerked his chin and clicked his own tongue.

'And you're right. I haven't been well.'

She stared at him. 'I bet it's the way you're thinking. If you think ill it can make you ill. I'm sure that's right.'

'And where did you get an idea like that?'

'I worked it out of course. I'm not a complete nit. That's not to say there aren't some people who are really ill, but you look the kind of person who might be *making* it happen. I see it going on all the time. Polo?'

'No thanks.'

'I can push the tip of my tongue through the hole.'

He watched as she poked the mint into her mouth. A moment later it came out again, stuck there. She moved her tongue up and down. Whenever her gaze shifted from him, he'd risk looking at her damp, uncombed hair. It was smelling of wet leaves. His neck bristled. She looked up. The Polo was now making a small lump in her cheek and clicking against her teeth. The rain had almost died away. Leaves had been blown all over the carriageway. She began humming to herself, rocking her body in time to the melody. Had he been capable of it, Jim would have run away. The humming stopped. She swished the mint and swallowed saliva.

'That's it. An old worryguts. That's what you are.'

He rubbed his eyes. 'I don't think it's that simple,' he said. 'Though it would be great if it was. I mean there are reasons, factors, things, well, things I don't think you are old enough to understand.'

'Bullshit.'

He turned to her. A serious expression hung there for a moment before giving way to a smile. Jim looked at his knees, if only because it was a place he hadn't considered looking before. He was counting the silence. She was trying to tap the tips of her shoes against the seat and stroking her shins. He'd previously noticed how tight the skin was there, it's sheen.

'What's your name then?'

'Oh, Jim.'

She laughed. 'I don't know any Jims. Jims are dying out. Jims are like Jameses with no money. You must be quite old.'

'Compared to you I suppose I am.'

'I can't imagine being as old as that.'

Jim took another cigarette from his bag. She watched him light it, made some comment about his health. His hands were shaking and he was over-conscious of his heart-beat, the ache in his legs, the grumble of his guts and – in his forehead – a sensation of unreality as if a breath of wind could blow the world away. The girl along with it. The rain had stopped, though water was still patting against the roof of the shelter. He was cold and stiff and wanted to stretch himself, but there was no room and to a certain extent he was secured in his position by her eyes and his nervousness. He glanced at the soft line of her thighs.

'What shall we do then? If it doesn't come?'

'Of course it will come,' he said. 'There's no reason why it shouldn't. I expect it'll turn up with several more. You know what they're like.'

'No need to be nasty. You sounded really nasty then.'

'Sorry. I wasn't feeling nasty. Just the way it came out.'

'That's another thing about you older people. Something nasty underneath it all. Doesn't matter who they are.'

From the observation hole Jim saw a bus swing round the corner. The roar of it enveloped them and a cold wind blew through the shelter, billowing the hem of her skirt. Before he knew it she was jumping up and flapping her hand. At first it looked as if the bus wasn't going to stop, but when it was a few yards away they heard a clank of gears and a screech of brakes and watched it skid to a halt a few yards further along. A cloud of grey smoke belched from an exhaust pipe at its side. The girl ran ahead. Jim collected his bag and followed. There was a rush of air as the door opened and she jumped in. Jim had fixed his eyes on a small slit in the side of her skirt. A sliver of chicken skin was showing through. She had been right about the fare. Sixty-five pence was the maximum. He tendered the right money into the driver's grey hand. The bus was empty. The girl took a seat at the back and beckoned to Jim to join her. With a jerk of his head towards the rear-view mirror, the driver lurched the bus forward. The engine beneath them whined and vibrated. The driver was singing at the top of his voice – an old James Taylor number, all heartache and white blossoms. On the pavement ahead Jim fancied he saw a thin man with a bandage over his eyes who'd been hit by a car and was rolling round in agony, but it turned out to be a large piece of brown paper tied with white tape to a railing. He wanted to share his joke with the girl, but she was busy taking off her tie and undoing the buttons on her white blouse down to the V of her jumper. She coiled the tie neatly and put it into her blazer pocket. He was chewing the inside of his cheek and shaking his head. Through the trees he could see his old home, just the roof and half of the upstairs windows. The girl was pointing in the opposite direction to a small copse scattered with rocks close to a place where the stream ran over a weir. A large tree trunk lay along the bank.

'That's where I've been all afternoon. Down there. I sat on that log and brought my records up to date. I don't know what it is about the stream just there but I always think there's something magical about it. It's my *special* place. Do you know what I mean?'

Jim scratched his face. The bus was cold and uncomfortable and smelt of oil, old bus tickets, the sweat of yesterday's passengers.

There was a vision through a window once upon a time of an uncomplicated Autumn day, sunlight gold as it can be at that time of the year, the garden's greens and browns crystallised under a wet blue sky, a league of seagulls drifting homeward, the swing of nearby stems against the crimson maple, outlines of pale blue houses, tails of smoke, thinning poplars, but most of all *light*, which had draped a sense of motherhood over us all. Living could be seen for miles, gathering at the horizon to form a whole, and he'd been as wide as the view through his window and somehow at one with its mood, its season. He had little to do but watch. He had focused on games too frequently, too seriously, as if they were everything; yet in that instant he guessed they were nothing at all, nothing but the swing of a yellow leaf towards the brim of a weir. And much of it was plain nonsense. Calm would outlive practically anything. No matter if you lay in the devil's arms, so long as you owned serenity and could side-step that terrible beating. And this girl had no perfume other than the sweetness of chicken skin itself. We dream of being with it, naturally, though it isn't all of the dream even if we say so, for most of the time we are solitary creatures born with millstones of expectation and physical responses we have no courage for, aching instead for window moments few and far between. Of such capacity yet with so little substance.

The girl drew a creased photo from her inside blazer pocket.
 'That's me with the hat. And this is Mum. Can you see where we are?'
 'Yes. I love the hat.'
 'It was one of my birthday presents.'
 Having looked at it for a few moments, she returned the photo to her pocket and crossed her ankles. 'It was one of the nicest days I can remember. Everything was exactly right,' she said.
 'Yes.' Jim folded his arms.
 The bus had turned off the main carriageway and

was struggling up a steep hill among the houses of a new estate. At the top it took a rough track along the fringe of the wood till it reached a second road. The driver then accelerated down the hill, holding the steering wheel at arm's length, laughing to himself. In the rear-view mirror Jim saw the wide hollow of his toothless mouth. They had passed several deserted stops and the roads were generally free of other vehicles, giving the driver a certain confidence as he threw the bus round corners or accelerated through changing traffic lights. Only once had there been a hint of anyone on the streets at all, and then it was only the heel of a shoe drifting into the shadow of an alley running alongside a church. Lights were beginning to show in passing windows. The streetlamps were glowing yellow. There was a suggestion of darkness in the air. Above a hill in the distance he saw the first of the stars mustering a brightness of its own. The bus had taken a second detour along a dim lane thick with trees either side and barely wide enough for a vehicle of any kind to pass through. Twigs from the trees scraped against the windows and roof. In a small parking area to the left of the lane several cars with misted windows were parked around a snack trailer which had been shuttered up for the day. Jim couldn't remember having seen this part of town before and frequently glanced at the girl's face to check her expression. Invariably his look strayed to the triangle of skin showing where her blouse had been unbuttoned. Coming out of the trees they passed a circular house with battlements and minute leaded windows, its brickwork aflame with virginia creeper.

Her hand suddenly came to rest on his knee. 'We're about half way there,' she said.

'Where do you have to get off?'

'I was just thinking I might walk some of the way now the rain's stopped. The bus goes right to our house but I'm not in the mood. I like having time to think. If we get off a few stops before I know somewhere that does coffee. I quite often go there. They won't let me have it at home. Fancy that?'

Jim looked forwards. 'I don't mind. I might as well do that as anything else I suppose.'

The black hat and dark glasses of the driver were bobbing in tune with a new but unsung melody. The bus had passed through the pillared gateway of a crematorium and was moving quickly between rows of black and silver tombstones which lay among dozens of birch trees. At the far side of the crematorium they sped through a similar gateway, then swung upwards along the foot of a hill with trees to one side and the brightening lights of the town on the other. In a clearing on the right stood a public house with red and yellow fairy lights strung along its front. The curtains in its windows were drawn.

The girl turned to him and was patting his leg. 'Come on. Buck up, chuck.'

Jim's hands had become set in his lap. His palms were hot.

'We've been saying that all week at school. Buck up, chuck! Funny isn't it? I love things like that.'

Once again she was drawing her feet up, trying to rest them on the edge of the seat, the skirt slipping along her thighs as she did so. Once she'd accomplished it, Jim leaned away from her towards the window. The hand on his knee had become much heavier. As he crossed one leg over the other, her hand held on to maintain its position. It was the colour of clotted cream, smooth and unstained. He looked at her pale fingernails, the barely visible moons. Her fingers were finely proportionate to the size of her hand and were covered with minute lines woven one with the other. She was opening her knees and pushing them together, over and over. He looked out of the window. The bus was speeding down a road which curved to the right, following the hill's contours. In the headlights Jim caught briefly the eyes of an animal close to the ground beside a large tree.

The girl was sighing. 'You know what? I don't reckon anyone's going to catch this bus but you and me.'

'Doesn't look like it.'

'Perhaps he won't even bother to pull up when our stop comes.'

'Oh I'm sure he will.'

She laughed. 'I'm not so certain. Looks a bit grizzly, doesn't he?'

'It's just those dark glasses.'

'I can't stand people who wear sunglasses all the time. I mean, what's the point?'

At the bottom of the hill the road stretched straight for half a mile between rows of bungalows. Beyond them Jim could see the dark gleam of the river. At the end of the road the bus turned into an alley between a pair of industrial buildings and wound through several work-yards before reaching a narrow metal bridge with wooden sleepers as its base which the wheels thumped over. At the far side of the river they came into another yard lined with racks of stacked metal bars. Beyond the yard, in a narrow street made yellow by lamplight, stood a second public house, its frosted windows decorated with the names of ales. Thick wooden buttresses supported the front wall.

Though the girl had given up mentioning shrinkage, she frequently pointed through the window at unspoken things he took to be examples of it. Darkness was now hanging among the telegraph wires, and at ground level there were patches of mist the driver would rush through without slowing down. The bus was now climbing away from the river towards a regular network of detached houses, a part of town with a quietness and a self-determination about it. Here, Jim imagined, families played with calculators behind rich maroon curtains. And throughout his imagination the hand lay on his leg, following wherever he chose to move, refusing to slip off even as the bus careered round bends or turned abruptly into side-roads. Her skirt had slipped as far as it could and lay there in soft buckles around the tops of her finely textured legs. He refused to look at her except when she asked a question or made a comment. But he knew the smell of her well enough.

Suddenly the bus lurched to the left . Its nearside wheels mounted the pavement and both he and the girl were thrown forwards as the brakes were jammed on.

The driver sat upright in his seat. 'All change please.'

Jim thought that he must have misheard and quietly adjusted his position, noticing that at last the girl's hand had fallen away.

'All change. Let's be having you.'

She leaned into the aisle. 'But we're not there yet.'

Keeping his back to them but angling his head towards the mirror, the driver shrugged. 'Not my problem miss. This is where I stop.'

She looked at Jim. 'He's nuts.'

'All change ladies and gentlemen, *please*.'

Jim stood, zipping his waxed jacket and gathering his bag. The girl remained in her place, holding onto the chrome rail of the seat in front.

'But I don't think you should be pulling up here. We're almost as far from my stop as we were when we started.'

'Perhaps you've caught the wrong fucking bus miss. This is where I turn round and from here I go back the way I came.'

Jim was helping her to her feet. 'Come on. Don't make a fuss. He's obviously not with it.'

Taking Jim's hand, the girl led him down the centre of the bus. As they approached the steps the driver twisted a lever which opened the air-doors. They climbed down to a moist pavement. The door seemed to suck itself shut after them and immediately the bus pelted away from the pavement and accelerated along the road in the direction it had been going.

Jim released his hand. 'Where are we?'

'I think it's more or less this way,' she said.

He waved her forwards, indicating she should lead. They were in a narrow avenue which wound downwards before curving out of view. Houses at either side appeared to be asleep. A wedge of the black river marked by yellow light was just visible at the end of the road. And as darkness became more marked the street lamps glowed with a new ferocity, burning his eyes. Cold traces of mist hung in the air like scraps of gossamer. Turning to him, she held out her hands, shrugged and walked forwards, pretty as spring. Having dried out, her hair was buoyant, bobbing with every step she took. Frequently she paused and waited for him to catch up. He was particularly breathless now, feeling as old as Innisfree itself but not yet so beautiful, not yet so significant, nor with such an accumulation of grace. He strained after her, lead weights to his feet and thighs, something gnawing at his guts, a cold sweat in his underarms and all the tucked ugliness of which a man is capable. As she waited for him she'd maybe lean against a wall or post-box, smiling patiently, rolling strands of hair in her fingers. He was following the smell of her like a homeless dog. At the next junction they stood by an electricity sub-station debating which way to go. She suggested this way; he that. But finally he allowed himself to be guided by her greater clarity. As she walked on he reached for her coat to slow her down. She stopped. He found himself coming close, following the bumps of her spine from the small of her back to her neck. Faint but classical there, beneath realms of clothing. Streetlight had turned her skin a warm yellow and his breath was as cold as the sparkle of stars.

'You're going too fast,' he said. The whole of his chest was sore and his breathing was accompanied by melodies of phlegm. The road stretched onwards with nothing in sight but more narrowing pavements, more cold privets, more cramped gardens, awful fucking homes with unwelcome expressions, knots of tight roses clinging to trellis-work, and below them blue fishpools gleaming dark. She had retrieved his hand and was rubbing it to warm him up though in a dream he pulled aside her right arm, lay it around his waist, slid against her and looked at her mouth. The lips were parted a little; he caught a glimpse of her teeth, the tip of her tongue, the gleam of saliva. In surprise she stepped backwards against a hedge. He moved with her till a pain between his legs made him buckle down and fall to the pavement, the left corner of his mouth striking a grey slab. He could do nothing but listen to the click of her crimson shoes hurrying into the dark.

Thursday

i

Rubble under the mattress was making him uncomfortable, although he could minimise it by lying corner to corner. Several times he'd adjusted himself but a slope in the ground invariably brought his upper half to the wrong side and pulled his legs away from the mattress altogether. The edge at which his torso terminated had caught some of yesterday's rain despite the garage overhang, and his spells of sleep had been interrupted by the cold of it against his cheek. Now he smiled to himself and rolled onto his back. The lips of a precocious winter were kissing his face and brushing through his hair. He wasn't able to open his eyes. It was as if the skill to do so were being squandered between his brain and the eyes themselves. He could raise his brows but the bottom edge of his eyelids wouldn't unstick. The more effort he put into this the worse the problem became, tiddely-pom. He reached for covers that weren't there, forgetting in a thrill of semi-consciousness his exact predicament. From somewhere nearby, he could hear the voice of a disc-jockey – not individual words but a general enthusiasm culminating in a love song by Smokey Robinson and the Miracles. From his right came the rumble of heavy traffic. He reached for the plastic bag, his hand coming into contact with housebricks, scraps of wood and, right beside the bag itself, a stinging nettle. As he lit the cigarette his eyes finally opened to a landscape of grey. Looking first one way, then another, he saw the wet pebble-dash surface of the garage wall and a tangle of saplings. The saplings hung ghost-like from a low bank. Almost every leaf had fallen now. He could smell them, visualise them, listen to them almost. It was crossing his mind to be irritable but a bout of coughing at his first deep inhalation prevented this. Immediately above, he could see nothing but the indifference of a freezing fog. It was this rather than the sensation of cold which made him shiver. Twisting on to his side to rest on one elbow, it was coming to him why he'd woken so irrevocably this time. He climbed off the mattress, stumbled over the carpet of rubble and urinated into the wet saplings. A thick steam rose into the fog. Other than his immediate surroundings there was little to see but a blush of light apparently hanging in mid-air. A streetlamp or bedroom window. *Dear Miriam, sorry I couldn't make my death. Something came up.* Brushing back his hair, he lay down again to finish his cigarette. Music was still weaving through the fog. Only tramps slept on mattresses at the back of pebble-dashed garages. Only tramps. A wren was singing. And the beast was irrepressible. No sooner had he woken than it sprang to attention like a corporal enthusiastic for square-bashing. Hup-two-three-four! Like all tramps he had an explanation prepared which would distinguish him from others in this category: he'd fallen on hard wives. Now even the pockets of his waxed jacket were damp. Fat lot of good it had been trying to garb himself like poor Princess-less Mr Phillips. Presumably the only differences for royalty were having more rooms into which to scarper in the first place and being able to shield one's head against a higher quality of flying china: look out, here comes the Worcester soup tureen with pseudo oriental hand-painted figures fishing round a stork-crowded lake. The discjockey began again as Jim finished his cigarette and clambered through the line of saplings. He reached an area of grass surrounded by walls of fog impenetrable after five or six yards. The grass had been temporarily whitened. Each inhalation filled his lungs with the chill of day and he was one of many villains stalking this buckled underworld, longing for an Old Sumatran. Dreams and imagination are there to pad out an otherwise routine existence and it was kissing Miriam's underarms he remembered, a stubble where she'd razored them and an aluminium dryness from traces of roll-on. Walking to the left he came across a high, red-bricked wall with crumbled biscuit-coloured mortar and small felt-tip messages. He followed the wall, almost falling at a place where the grass dipped suddenly, then stooped through another line of saplings. A few yards further on the wall adjoined a summer house made of similar brick. High above him was a white window flecked with moving shadows: some jolly novelist, perhaps, plucking insignificant moments from thin air. Just beyond the summer house the wall moved at ninety degrees to the right. In the distance he could hear running water. The bank below the wall gradually narrowed till there was nothing left to walk on and he was forced to scramble down the slope through thickets of elder to a fast-running blue and silver stream with stepping stones. He crossed and climbed a bank on the other side, coming to a second wall which he followed till it ended abruptly with a white pillar. Turning to his right he wandered across an expanse of green, wondering when any of it would ever end, wondering how much information it was necessary to gather before a chap could begin to shine and one's remembered fruit woman was irrevocably drawn to the light. I remember your mouth as if you were yesterday. Remember the loops of your blue dungarees.

The sound of traffic became louder. After a few minutes he noticed a disturbance of the fog brought about by a complexity of slow-moving headlamps. He turned away from them till the noise lessened and the disturbance could no longer be seen. Moments later he came to a footbridge which took him to a second path winding beneath a line of mature birch trees. Every twenty paces a cocoon of fog would be picked out by the orange glow of a wayside lamp. He was experiencing a slight but widespread pain throughout his body. At a fork in the pathway he found a bench and decided to wait. Have another cigarette. After ten minutes or so a clump of blue-coated schoolgirls shuffled past him, laughing over something that hadn't happened the night before. He nodded to them, hoping they wouldn't draw false conclusions once out of earshot. Gradually the fog above him, if not that at ground level, lightened somewhat and became tinged with hints of sunlight which now and then found a way to the grass at the other side of the path, and the gilded strands of dew-laded webs strewn among it. He may have been hungry. It was difficult to decide. In all several dozen schoolgirls came by, each with a dark beret. Bag of books. White, mist-whispered skin. As his surroundings cleared he made out an ochre coloured wall and the side of a house skirted by the path.

Twenty minutes later he stretched himself and walked on, following the path in to the back of a cul-de-sac where a long terrace of houses shrank into the distance, each with a uniform back garden and each becoming golden as a risen sun burnt off the fog. He saw rabbit hutches, footballs left from yesterday, sheds with dark windows and steaming felt roofs. Mothers hanging out washing in cramped, irritable gardens with cracked central paths, dying vegetable patches and dark, tired lawns. The houses seemed too tall in proportion to their widths. Half a dozen radios, mostly tuned to the same channel, were throwing music from opened kitchen doors. In one garden a man was coming up the path holding a pint mug and a sheaf of papers. He looked guilty. A liquid in his mug was steaming. Catching sight of Jim, he bowed his head. There were toddlers on doorsteps, wives in upper windows, cats curled on wet mats, dogs snuffling through compost heaps, and those first unharmonised yawns of a waking town.

Jim was shivering still. He pushed his hands into the damp pockets to try to warm them and made a decision to turn downhill at every junction or – where it wasn't clear whether there was a slope in the road or not – to go right. Each road he came across was named after a tree or a dead politician. The suburbs had become repopulated with traffic, hurrying pedestrians, angry-faced lollipop persons, dogs without collars. Soon after reaching a main carriageway, a stout woman in a black and white overcoat took him by the arm and squeezed a pound coin in his hand. He tipped what would have been his hat and thanked her, carrying on for another half-mile or so, stopping frequently to gather strength and, at one point, crouching in someone's driveway to avoid the attentions of a pair of roaming policewomen. Following a thrash on the head from a wet sponge thrown by the house-owner, he experienced a clear vision of Laura stumbling along a deeply-mudded track; could hear her voice and remember the way she looked from over here where the bank was drier. He had been wondering if he might climb a tree and was testing coils of ivy which surrounded the trunk right up to the first branch. She was holding out her arms. Laura one warm afternoon, soft green rocks on the bank beyond her. This was more like it. Laura and her densely-spun overcoat, black wellingtons, a squelching as she moved uneasily forwards. He crossed the hump of land to watch as she came round the corner, wishing to see her as she would have been. By herself. The sun and autumn had softened the forest floor. Beneath her shoes were twigs, fallen cones, the soft reds of yewberries. We weren't going anywhere particularly and there were still traces of moon in her hair where it hung from her bobble hat. Earlier she'd chased me with a hazel switch for temporarily refusing to accept the miniature white vase she'd brought, and I was formulating theories over brevity and the capacity it has for preventing disorder: disorder, that is, of words and the spirit they convey.

Jim was catching sight of his own reflection in the windows of an approaching phone box. She wouldn't take too kindly to him now, by heaven. This rapidly developing vagrancy and chaos of opinion. He pulled open the door of the kiosk and rested against its interior. With the door closed, both sides of the kiosk touched his shoulders and he was forced to bend his knees a little to accommodate himself. He pushed some coins into the slot and watched the amount register on the digital display. Though he hadn't considered who to phone, his fingers tapped out the number of the Benefit Office. After half a dozen rings, Mei Lee answered. Deepening his voice slightly, he asked for Jeff. Through the dim pane level with his eyes he could see a junction up ahead leading to the avenue where Miranda lived. A few yards along it he could just make out the roof of the pavilion, or whatever it was that he'd seen from her kitchen the day before.

'Jeff? It's me, Jim.'

'Jim! How are you?'

'Fine. Absolutely fine. How about you?'

'Actually I'm on top of the . . . Sorry. I mean . . .'

'Don't start that. Hold on. There's a juggernaut going past, bloody things.'

'What?'

'Never mind.'

Jeff was half whispering. 'Where are you then?'

'In a phone box.'

'I thought they brought them round on trolleys these days.'

'No, I'm not at the hospital. I've come out for a while.'

'But you're . . . not well. Surely they didn't . . .'

'Oh, I'm OK. Listen. It's about tonight. I don't think I'll be there when you . . .'

'Sorry? It's that traffic again. Hey! You'll never guess what. I've done it, Jim. Done it. *And* I've thrown out the shirt.'

'Done what?'

'Yesterday morning. That chat we had the other

day really did me a power of good. I ran all the way back here, marched right up to Mei Lee and asked her out. And – can you believe it – she said yes, Jim. No hesitation. I think you were right when you said she might have been waiting for me to pop the question. She was very shy, mind you. Very shy. I think she would have blushed if she'd been more our sort of colour. Anyway, once she'd said yes I didn't know what to do with myself. I'd been expecting her to tell me to go away. I was the bravest I'd ever been. And I hate to say this, but when we got round to the subject of trousers it turned out they were one of the things she first liked about me. I melted, Jim. Melted. Course, they're all taking the mickey out of me here – aren't you? And I'm really nervous. I haven't eaten since. Tonight's our first date so I won't be able to come and see you I'm afraid. Yesterday I managed to get a couple of tickets for *The Tempest*. I thought it would be a good introduction to our culture, you know?'

Jim was picking at a taxi advertisement which had been stuck to the coin box. 'That's wonderful Jeff. I was about to cancel your visit anyway, but it looks like I don't have to.'

'No, no. Sorry. I was going to come Friday instead. Will you be back at the hospital by then?'

'I don't think so.'

'So, are you on your way home?'

'No, I've . . . '

Jeff was speaking with an unfamiliar confidence. 'Why not for heaven's sake? You should get yourself indoors. Keep warm. Does Miriam know where you are?'

'Well, not exactly, but . . . '

'Then ring and let her know. She must be worried

sick. Do you want me to come over and take you home?'

Only three of the taxi number's digits remained. 'Don't worry about it. I'm all right. I just happen to be ringing. I don't *want* anything. Listen, I hope you have a great time at the theatre. Remember to be cool. Absolutely cool. Don't whatever you do tell her you'd like to lie in the gutter for her or anything like that. It won't work. They like you to do it if the chips are down, but till then they prefer you to keep the whole idea quiet.'

'You think so?'

'Definitely.'

'Well, you're a bit late actually, but she didn't seem to mind. In fact she told me she'd never heard anything quite like it. I gave her the Quality Street to back it up. I think this is it at last, old friend.'

'Certainly looks that way.'

'And it's mainly thanks to you. I'm sorry if I'm talking about myself again. I start off on the right foot but then something happens. I meant it when I said you should get back home. Put your feet up by the hearth and all that.'

Jim suddenly heard Jacobson's voice: 'Are you going to be on that phone all day? Clients will be trying to get through and, in case you hadn't noticed, all the other phones are engaged with *bona fide* calls.'

'Oh, hang on to your horses! Anyway Jim, looks like I'm going to have to call it a day. Please do what I've said. Ring me once you're at home if you like. Oh, and guess what? On Saturday we're going to a Vietnamese restaurant to see what sort of food her type eat. She's had mongrel in the past. Can you imagine that? Whole new worlds are opening up for me Jim. Whole new worlds.'

There was a click on the line followed by the dialling tone. Jim replaced the receiver and rested his head against the list of international codes. He wanted to fall asleep but was brought to his senses by a nun who flew from the newsagent's opposite, then beat her palms against the kiosk windows in a horror of black and white.

ii

The pavilion was situated on raised ground overlooking a garden of remembrance surrounded – other than at the entrance – by a conifer hedge six or seven feet high. By now the sun had burnt off the fog, though daylight itself came filtered through a veil of high cloud which spoke of less clement weather to come. On a circular concrete dais in the middle of the garden stood a black marble statue of a woman dancing, her graceful lines and slim figure reminiscent of art deco porcelain. From the dais a number of gravel paths fanned outwards to a broad paved walkway. In between the paths lay well-tilled flowerbeds scattered with shrubs and evergreens, but planted for the most part with grey green wallflowers in preparation for spring. At this far end a low flight of flagstone steps led to a lawn and the pavilion itself, with its narrow verandah and an old wooden bench painted green. Though access to the interior of the pavilion was barred by a locked door, Jim could sniff its emptiness through cracks in a pair of shuttered windows either side.

He sat down on the brightest half of the bench where the wet from melted frost had almost dried. From this raised position he could see Miranda's living room window, her flecked blue curtains and, among shadows of a reflected sky, a veil of interior walls. Perhaps he'd come too far. Expected too much. He stretched his legs and yawned. Eased a stiffness in his neck by twisting his head back and forth. The garden itself was entirely free of litter, as if something of common sanctity was being honoured here that no one would wish to desecrate. The rain-washed gravel paths had been meticulously weeded, while the naked shrubs and gleaming evergreens either side gathered weak sunshine and scattered it over the soil. At the bottom of the flagstone steps was a young tree with deep red leaves, most of which had fallen across the broad walkway. He would have brought Laura here to see them. Settled next to her on this same bench. Held conversations with no sense of having to outwit her or prove her mistaken. Such were her dreamtimes he quietly enjoyed her through and through. Her words and eyes like suns themselves. The beautiful is more often remembered than lived. It usually comes about at some time other than now, there to recall as a comforter on less satisfying days: pictures, snapshots, moments of clarity, their displeasures removed. A cure through time of gut-pains, the indigestions brought about by a realisation of abandoned possibilities. The nausea of risk and cold skies. Yes, she'd been at the top of a flight of cobbled steps against a clear moon and Old Sumatran sky whilst the invalid hauled himself towards her, clinging to the iced iron rail and looking up now and then to catch moon kisses in her cobweb skirt, his fingers white spiders. Below him in the unlit road stood her car, and beyond it a park, lime-green with frost, its footpaths tinted slugtrails, the silhouettes of spirits caught against a blaze of townlight further on.

She'd taken the steps three at a time. Snaps of cold leg in the thrill of her skirt. All he'd had to do was reach the top. The cobbles had become uneven with a hewing of time. Over there a watchful man had brought two alsatians to sniff among the sycamores. Laura in frost, and a challenge with no victor. Coming closer he saw the line of her jaw, traces of silver in her eyes, her slightly parted lips pink and infinitely kissable; and he was thinking of himself as some poor metaphor for the myth of his decisive brotherhood. And there were tales to cook up for the morrow, narratives to establish, alibis to create of suitable unlikeliness.

An elderly couple were coming through the gate, their fingers delicately linked, one white head bobbing in opposition to another, thinning silver hair. She was wearing a thick woollen shawl, he an unzipped brown jacket. With a glance towards Jim's sacrilegious hairstyle they made their way down one of the fanned pathways to stand below the statue of the dancing lady, talking in wrinkled whispers to one another while reaching out to touch the black marble feet, a flash of gold on the woman's finger, a second flash on his. They paid respects, turned and walked back towards the gate, slowly and in step, pointing to shrubs of interest. Conferring. Tramps could always afford cigarettes. And you put a bench down for frail old dears to think of Gallipoli and it's immediately occupied by someone who can't be bothered. Someone with whiskers and a plastic bag. Someone who used to be a human being but gave it up as a shallow political statement. Another bugger on a no-good bench. Someone with drifting lifestyle but an exact routine – library for one hour from opening time, then up the street to gather coins from conscience-striken capitalists; over to the museum for a spell by the bronze-age radiator, then off to catch a falling star in gardens of remembrance. Thinking back to those more laundered days when one danced to more popular tunes.

You were ever the best of playmates and adversaries, Oswald – white, petrified, marching Godward – and though your diary must have outlined dreams of those Israelite girls, Samantha and her sisters ended up inviting less laboured chaps to tea, chaps who wouldn't look dicks in white napkins. You were no match for the girls' fluency, the liquid of their afternoons, their heaven legs. You returned to days of bubble-gum, scrumping the apples of immobile pensioners, playing tag along the minnow stream, sharing a Gold Leaf behind the printing works or encouraging me to throw soil at Bumper Daniels as his search continued life-long for evil boys. And my poems wouldn't ripen, too much arrogance and the imagination of ungoosed limbs inapplicable to any human coming into our shadow.

Most of this has been dedicated to those who know, those who *knew*. Those who do know will know who they are while those who don't won't, and will slip anxiously to the next scrap of information which is: Oswald, I disliked you but loved you, and you are surely the most remembered friend whichever way those sentiments settle. Never again will the otherwise skilled hands of the Great Potter throw such an unlikely vessel. Though you have tiptoed into the future I remember you as a nose with a boy hanging awkwardly round it, and it is as a nose you will make your way through living, and it will be a nose which decides whether you discover anything other than Gospel pleasures. Maybe it has assisted you, that excessive nasal influence, since it no doubt prevented fruition of evil dreams which might have spoilt your reputation with God. And did your hair need to be so brief and curly at the neck? And couldn't you have found a solution to the unreasonable gap between your neck and shirt collar? What villains your shirt-purchasing parents must have been. And then your legs, hopeless for football, as if vital bones were missing, leading you – rather than the ball – to be smacked into the net by bullies wearing Pumas. Those poor legs more suited to the playing of fops in Shakespeare than to the ambitions of a harmless boy in twentieth century England. Only when you donned purple hosiery in the school play did they seem justified at all. At the time, you'll remember, our friendship was further consolidated by my continued use of your correct name while shaving boys about us were slandering you as the Dancing Dipstick, most probably because of those effeminate quadrilles. Time insists I should let go of you now. May your God go with you in the absence of Oswald-loving angels. It is with regret I conclude that, though you were always on the brink of making your mark as a child, you have been of little or no significance here. If you happen to read this volume then I would hope to bolster your courage and self-esteem with our childhood battle-cry. Surely you remember it?

A line of cloud with veils of rain falling from its leading edge had appeared above Miranda's flat and was moving ever closer at a speed disproportionate to the gentle breeze. Just a few minutes later the first spots patted against the pavilion roof. The dancing statue soon glistened. Climbing to his feet, Jim wandered up and down in rehearsal for a haunting, some poor damn ghost, his hair sculpted with grease, nose constantly down his insides to smell himself. Miranda's curtains had become a kind of symbol: that liberty had its times of cruelty too. Instinctively he lurched backwards, then laughed aloud as a bird swooping from nowhere thumped in to the bench and fell soft against the verandah.

   Moisture. That's it. When loving no longer makes moisture the dream is somehow coming to its end and days themselves dry up, become impenetrable so you can't fuck them, no moisture to release, lubricate, glisten, loosen, soften you, your thighs locked tight against his spirit. Then quickly-moving cloud covered the sky and from the heavens other birds were racing across its greyness, as if to sanctuary. Having reluctantly performed a few simple exercises to unlock his joints, Jim gathered the bird, carried it by its legs to the nearest flowerbed, scooped a hole in the wet soil, and carefully buried it. As he returned to the verandah he took off his waxed jacket and rolled it in to a ball, which he tucked at the far end of the bench before lying down, making sure he still had a clear view of Miranda's curtains.

iii

Yes. Well I found myself laughing at the whole thing once I'd put the soil over the bird you know the whole thing gates in the rain dribbles running round the wrought iron whorls the dancing woman too as if she were truly dancing though I knew she couldn't be not in this weather anyway something in her skirt a diaphanous black marble and the smile some sculptor had carved there as if to say *I'll crucify the meek of heart* the sculptor that is knowing I'd be coming here dreaming up Laura out of season conjuring her hamster cheeks her Nirvana hand those sips at the corners of her mouth we often followed with our tongues on vanilla afternoons dribbles of it drying there as she had her life in an old Gladstone bag pulling it out to show me in the jade shade of an old Scots pine a diary a paperweight a poem by someone I hadn't heard of her knees risen glimpses of the underworld wrapped in scarlet not Miss Scarlet as in Cluedo nor her namesake Captain but knicker-scarlet plump with secrecy the underworlds unfucked while down in the valley guides were dib-dibbing all over the sward and a distant goat had eaten a circle of verge the extent of its chain that's it when you put a goat on a chain it eats the grass within chewing distance and nothing more till the great keeper comes to shift it and later there was an episode where she ran along the horizon leaping in parody of silken dancers her arms held out traces of hair in their pits the crimson T-shirt laundered but bobbing out of synchronisation revealing aspects of her skin to workmen had they been coming by which they weren't because this was the countryside one stolen summer day when bees had abandoned the innumerable elms for heathland honey and tangs of heather her skirt too splashing up her thighs the browns and softs of them just ripe for this bastard's hand which was honing in on an imagination of them the same afternoon we ended up driving through the blue green hills with mirror lakes in cups below the white and reds and dogs of picnickers a wonderment of families beside the willow trees while above we were finding ruined churches made of blue-black stone old milk churns village greens where simpletons once stood in stocks country mansions howling with peacocks or irrefutable evidence of Laurie Lee poor soul has a more pastoral reputation than he bargained for sagging pubs with clematis round the door and in her life-bag there were sandwiches too bread with nowt taken out and vegetarian paste which was fine except it made us thirsty with tortilla chips for afters adding to the problem so we shared a bottle of Aqua Libra she'd brought and ended up bloated as pigs despite the restoration of our alkaline balance as described by the label then in a hollow by a stone cross we came upon a remote bookshop tended by a nervous young man who thankfully wasn't her type with white skin and eyes in the back of his head to make sure kids didn't colour in *The Lorelei* or ruin his family Bibles and he was a short stocky chap not the type one associates with books books of many shapes and sizes first editions by Aldous Huxley oh what a daft name hand-coloured volumes of poetry books on wooden ships yaks subterfuge in the USSR Anthony Wedgewood Benn before he became one of us toadstools what you could eat or couldn't eat how to make your own bunker out of sheets of metal provided you had a spade at the moment of crisis a History of the Kurds photograph compilations of the Royal Family from 1902 Laura said it was about time the whole brylcreemed sequinned lot of them got their comeuppance and handed over the cash *Recipes for Rabbit* a rare edition signed by the author as if anyone gave a tuppenny damn the first chapter was how to skin them so she left that well alone almost making a complaint to the short chap with the white skin who that day was sporting an unenviable carbuncle evoking her sympathy and thus prompting her to buy *How to Find Out What's Not Nice About Yourself Then Fucking Get Away With It* or something like that her cobweb skirt miraculous amongst the dust and spines and wooden floors I spent almost as much time looking at the stoops of her leg or sunlight coming through cracked windows on to her neck or the way her lips moved as she read through titles to herself I could see the white chap watching her too though he was pretending to value a set of six volumes some old lady with a wicker basket and mushroom lips had just brought in probably the last thing of her late husband's to be exchanged for cash and then bacon in the village butchers and each time Laura lowered herself to the lower shelves her skirt giggled along her thighs and I was hoping to spot a flaw in her character something she might say or do but I couldn't not on that afternoon at least we could tell the chap with the bookshop was having cash flow problems the way he sent the old dear packing with her volumes baconless what is it with this world where an old woman can't have a pound of streaky I was so unimpressed I almost disliked Mr Kiam that's it we were waiting for contentment to prove erroneous for ecclesiastical thunderbolts the wagging of Jesus' finger or for the ground to crack open and swallow us and later that same afternoon we were lying on the crest of a long barrow looking directly into the blue the earth rocking beneath us and he was unable to touch you even though stinks of Miriam and the zoo-man were coming in on the breeze like the hop-skip giggles of children at parties with off cake and flat lemonade oh that's not to say he didn't hold your hand or twist his blue remembered head to watch your ear but he wouldn't fall wouldn't fall your ear all pink whorls and strands of lemonade hair your smell the smell of barns shadows moist spring bridlepaths the white of your arms thrown back the smooths of your legs parted slightly Whittington shoes splaying open ankles for a kiss a jet roaring over practising for the next crisis which wouldn't be *our* crisis not really since all we did was dream of J.B.Priestley teas cucumber sandwiches wicker chairs Piccadilly infusions in bone china cups and associated wonders lying there like upturned woodlice on the ridge of the barrow and by the time we'd finished not doing anything your nose had turned red in the sun and you'd hoisted your skirt to get a blush to your thighs and for a laugh you said *I spy with my little eye something beginning with S* and by that time he'd started peppering his guesses with four-letter words to thrill himself and make out he was now impervious to sentiment but you weren't fooled voicing the opinion he was as tough as a toasted teacake a wonder of bashfulness soaking up sunlit days or hiding as now in a wet garden all tuckered out and tucked up on a bench by the pavilion gaining some protection from its overhang with prayers for a fluency he'd put aside in favour of the unremarkable and now the price was seering like a bodkin through an arras into his belly-o.

He woke thinking of these things.

iv

He'd been asleep too long. The sky had darkened and the rain was falling as a wind-blown mist which, though not heavy, soon soaked his hair and ran down his face. He was licking trickles of it as he crossed the garden and glanced up at her blue curtains in time to see them being pulled across. In lighted rooms below, the guardians were at their places looking out, each of them as motionless as a corpse, and though he knew they couldn't see him he bowed his head and turned up his collar; made his way down the cul-de-sac to the main road convinced, for some reason, he'd forgotten something, though he couldn't think what it was. Forgotten something . . . and he wouldn't be able to live it down. The traffic had snarled up in all directions and both rain and cloud and the dying of the afternoon had prompted drivers to turn on their headlights, which wasted against the boots of cars in front and spilt into the wet road surface. Brake-lights were reddening swabs of exhaust fumes as tempers frayed and he could see drivers hunched in their seats, some crouching forwards over steering wheels to make room for their heads, others leaning through windows to make sure they didn't scrape the sides of cars coming in the opposite direction, their progress otherwise hampered by humps and buckles in the road surface, tarmac cracked like wounds, the cacophonous panic of wanting to rush home or rush out of town. The off-side wheels rolled tight against the kerb, squealing as a result, crushing whatever litter had been thrown there. As he waited for a space he couldn't escape the idea that the guardians had now spotted him and were gazing down without smiles in condemnation of him. Four of them, already in white nightwear, hands folded at their breasts. The line of traffic would rattle for a few moments, then slide forward. Tired of waiting, Jim moved quickly between two cars to the middle of the road, causing the second driver to sound his horn and scream abuse. A car crawling the other way brushed against his coat then almost caught his foot with its rear wheel. He acknowledged the blare of the next car with the flat of his hand and crossed to the kerb. Dimly coloured clouds were moving too quickly overhead. And gardens bordering the highway were so much smaller than he remembered, it was like a joke floundering at the punch-line. Water was rolling from the sleeve of his waxed jacket, down the back of his hand into the plastic bag, too empty with its pointless book and packet of cigarettes. Yes, the house under whose windows he stood wasn't quite as he remembered it, neither as tall nor as wide, with a shorter front garden and a black gate whose hinges were rusted up. He passed through it, looking up as the fucking guardians crooned down and his legs – as if sensing an imminent rest, a long rest – wanted to buckle under him, pre-empt the occasion, and he was kind of warning them to hold out. As he reached the door a shower of water from a blocked guttering smacked against his head and shoulders but the whole predicament did nothing but amuse him, make him smile. He was like that, Jim. Having pressed the doorbell, he stepped back with a dread he might collapse, though not entirely through weakness. He'd seen it all before in a moment of déjà vu of the kind that had troubled him for years, and now it made his heart race. He knew that whatever movement or expression he tried to avoid the sensation, the outcome would adapt to an old familiarity. His guts burned at the first thumps coming down the stairs. Some bastard on the road had squeezed through his car window to give a piece of his mind to the bastard behind who'd crunched against his bumper, but he'd become wedged half-way and had to struggle back and settle for a rage of his fists. Yes, the whole thing had become a poor joke with no rhyme or reason. And those thumpings were loud enough to make him cover his ears and hum to himself, as he'd done once upon a time to avoid noises from an outside world.

The door opened. His first reaction was to laugh. Miriam was having to bend her knees before she could look at him properly, the muscle at her jaw already in spasm, her head tilting away from the hall ceiling and her eyes clouding in that familiar way. Eventually she thumped to her knees, though even then she was filling much of the available space and had to press her hands above the door to support herself.

'Where the hell have you been?'

He was still smiling. By passing her weight to the right she was able to free her left arm, bend it appropriately and slide her fist towards him. As it came through the doorway the fist uncurled, allowing one finger to extend and poke at his shoulder. A heavy, cream-scented finger it was.

Her breath blew against his wet hair making him reluctant to reply for the moment.

'And where's the milk? Can't you remember anything? Where's the bloody milk?'

Jim was hastily constructing an alibi, wondering if he'd managed to disguise those moon-traces in his eyes. As Miriam inhaled, her shoulders heaved to their fullest extent and the floor creaked beneath her knees. Behind him, dominating sweeter sounds of traffic and running water, a church bell pealed for perhaps ten seconds and, after a moment's pause, struck the hour.